RED

Irwin Allan Sealy is the award-winning author of four novels, *The Trotter-nama*, for which he received a Commonwealth Writers' Prize, *Hero*, *The Everest Hotel* and *The Brainfever Bird*, as well as a travel book, *From Yukon to Yucatán*. He lives in the foothills of the Himalayas.

IRWIN ALLAN SEALY

RED

PICADOR

First published 2006 by Picador

First published in paperback 2007 by Picador
an imprint of Pan Macmillan Ltd
Pan Macmillan, 20 New Wharf Road, London N1 9RR
Basingstoke and Oxford
Associated companies throughout the world
www.panmacmillan.com

ISBN 978-0-330-41148-6

1 3 5 7 9 8 6 4 2

A CIP catalogue record for this book is available from
the British Library.

Printed and bound in Great Britain by
Mackays of Chatham plc, Chatham, Kent

To The Writer's Family

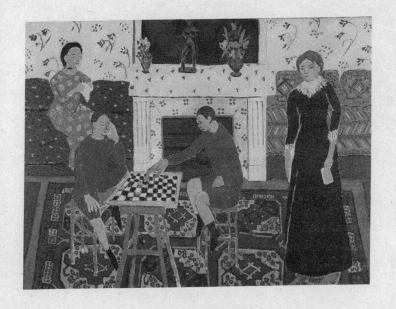

Henri Matisse, *The Painter's Family*, 1911

Contents

PART 1

Three Paintings

'The Red Room'

Red is sitting on a bench seat in front of the picture leaning forward elbows on knees chin cupped in both hands staring at the painting as if she could climb through the frame and vanish into it.

By now a museum guard trained to spot compulsives should have come up and stood casually by the next canvas ready to grapple with her and relieve her of the Stanley knife which somehow slipped through security. But at the moment the uniformed guards are elsewhere, padding to or from this room along the wide sunny corridor on the third floor of the Hermitage, Winter Palace of the Tsars.

And Red has no telltale tic, no giveaway bulge in boot or pocket. Nothing that shouts danger except leaves of flaming red hair. And a window of shell-pink skin opening at the small of her back.

There is only one other person in the Matisse room, this vestibule in what was once the apartments of the ladies-in-waiting. The room of waiting.

Zach is waiting for Red to move. He has looked at all the other paintings in the room except the one she's examining and doesn't want to go on to the next room in case he forgets to come back. Thoroughness is both his failing and his strength. When she won't move he goes and stands behind her, behind the backless bench, and looks with her at the painting.

He stands there a long time in his grey parka and moleskins one notch down from his body brown. Here is what he sees:

The Red Room by Henri Matisse

What it shows:

a room perfectly red, with a maid in black and white laying a table already set with a vase of flowers, decanters of red and white wine, assorted fruit. Two rush-plaited chairs up against the table, and a window to the left. Giant blue arabesques that swarm like serpents over tablecloth and wallpaper.

What it does not show:

The Fall of Icarus; Apollo and Daphne; The Beheading of St John the Baptist; The Annunciation of the Blessed Virgin Mary; The Count and Countess of Pujols; The Painter Himself; Etc.

What only I can show you:

the civet cat rustling this minute in the bamboo, here in our valley in the Himalayan foothills: when I looked up I saw its silhouette walk along the top of our brick folly, black against the neighbour's white tubelight. Here it is:

----------------------- imagine it -----------------------

RED

How exactly the silent flow of black hyphens across my screen as
I hold down the key replicates the progress of the cat!
Shoo!

The red room is not Matisse's own dining room in the family
house at Issy but simply a version of the room in an earlier
dinner-table painting. The maid is a version of an earlier model,
Matisse's former mistress, Caroline Joblaud, mother of his daughter. Ten years on, she reappears, her light hair an affront to the
dark-haired Madame Matisse. (The knife cut both ways: a year
after Caroline left, Madame Matisse's dark hair appeared in a new
version of the original light-haired *Woman Reading*.) The decanters are likely still around, the chairs perhaps still sat on by the
family Matisse.

Well, in the painting a table is being set, perhaps for guests,
perhaps simply for the family. Perhaps, perhaps. But the viewer is
not asked to meditate on the action in progress. He is not
concerned to ask, as with earlier paintings, for example:

Why is the ploughman's back turned to the falling Icarus?

What is Daphne saying to Apollo?

How must Salome feel as she watches the axe descend?

Can the dove that moans in the Blessed Virgin Mary's ear – for
she conceived her son through the ear, Zach, deaf in one
ear, was always intrigued to learn – *ever return in peace to
its high branch in the elm?*

Etc.

No, the viewer is invited to another feast. He is asked to
consider what one colour is saying to another, what one plane
(red tabletop) is handing its neighbour (red wall). He may touch
the tablecloth, he may not taste the fruit; he may tremble at the

windowpane, he may not pull up the sash and lean out of the window. Because there's nothing out there, just colour. The window is a painting within a painting.

The truth is the table is being set for the painter. He first set the maid setting the table. He set the room. Story – that string of perhaps – has here taken a new turn. Icarus, got up as the modern painter, has returned to punish the ploughman and shepherd who turned their backs on his fall. They thought they were the only ones with serious work on their hands.

In the window it is still spring to the room's summer, morning to the room's high noon. (In the sky it is still winter.) Apple blossom whitens the trees, meadow flowers dot the grass. A pink house from the heart of childhood stands on the nearest rise. The true horizon is not at the sky but in the room, the line where the table and wall meet.

How long Zach stands there meditating on the scene he's not sure in the end, but in the end here is what he sees:

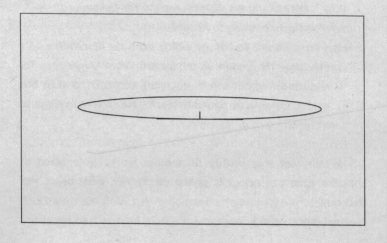

RED

He's not a scientist, so how the paradigm shifted he can't say. But a red shift there was. He's not a painter, so how the frame shifted he's not sure. He doesn't deal in the visual. (His work exists in another dimension, not in space, though more than anything he would like to make an absolute music that is free of time. A composer.)

All he knows is that at some point, in time, his gaze shifted from the painting on the wall to the woman in front of it.

>More specifically to the window in her back where the line of her top has ridden up as she leans forward and the line of her belt has ridden down.

>More specifically still to that short vertiginous line where the downy skin gullies in a fold of flesh more dizzying than any navel.

>Still more specifically to the thin red line of lace that appears to support the vertical.

Zach has lost his impatience: now he could stand there forever. Now the danger is that she'll move too soon. The red shift is what happens when light from outer space turns reddish, i.e. gets longer in the wave or is displaced redward in the spectrum implying recession (or imminent recession) in the celestial object. She could get up and go at any point in time and he'd be lost in space forever. He has two impulses:

1) to touch straight off, risk a scream a slap terror disgrace.
2) to stand mesmerized, then simply follow, covered in goose pimples.

1) is very close, so strong he has to fight himself, choking, actually choking. 2) is what he does, but loses her. Somewhere in that maze of galleries that is the Hermitage, Red makes her getaway.

Next day he's back.

'The Black File'

On the side of the next truck you pass you may see a certain painting, usually on the panel above the rear wheel. Sometimes too it will appear on the back of an autorickshaw, sometimes on the shutters of a village shop. The original is in a niche, one of twenty paintings on the facade of a ruin, once a rich merchant's house on the banks of the Tons river.

Six black figures walk singlefile under a nightdark sky.

White crescent moon, black pencil trees. A grey river murmurs, combed with reeds, a boat so long and low it would surely roll and tip out any cargo. The walkers pass it by. They follow a path, their legs so evenly spaced by the painter they could be shared, the legs of a mythical beast. The path snakes through bushes shaped like the club on playing cards towards a reddled house on a hill.

The one in front has a cobra head fanned open, the white spectacles-mark showing its double loop on the hood. Her forked tongue shivers blue in the moonlight.

The five men following are naked except for a black codpiece. Their hair is greased with the same pomade that slicks their skin. The codpiece could be armour on the many-legged creature; it passes between the buttocks and wraps around the bulge at the front before being tucked in tight at the waistband.

Borderless, the picture stares down the centuries, the niche its house and frame. Its remote ancestor, on the walls of a cave lost to the world in the Himalayan earthquake of 1991, might have been anywhere between thirty and forty thousand years old.

A draught streams from the niche of the painting. Go up close, feel its breath. Cool and moist it pours off the painted river. The lime-washed façade looks east; with every sunrise its reds flush and fade a little. Turn away, close your eyes. Let it live.

Bareheaded, blacksmeared, castemarked, the file of walkers shrinks from leader through led, the last in line the smallest. That is in place of perspective. This last one's head is saurian, widest at the jaw. His chin has a three-day growth, his teeth are ground down to even pegs. He has little rubber balloons pulled onto his fingertips. His shoulderblades glide in the moonlight, his hair is a ridge of hackles. Laundry blue and lampblack. From one side he looks like a chameleon walking upright; his hard sardonic eye takes your measure from a past impossibly remote. Notice how his forearms get no narrower than the lean upper arm. They could bind a woman fast or whip this young cypress out of the ground and strip it to a pole. He is a dreamer. When he is sad he hums a melody of four notes.

Come up close. Bring your ear to the niche.

Listen.

Preface to *Annals of The Black Codpiece Society*, E. T. (by permission), Dariya Dun, no date.

'The Painter's Family'

In a museum or gallery Zach will look until struck.

By some fragment that transfixes him, when he will close his eyes momentarily, receiving the arrow with the piety of St Sebastian, and then, unlike the bound saint, feel free to leave the place, no matter how far into it he's got. In the Hermitage, where foreigners pay ten times as much as natives, this is an inconvenient habit so he overlooks it. He has shut his eyes once already, on the Neva side after seeing a kingfisher blue from the twelfth century that went straight to his heart. It was an anonymous panel of the Virgin Mary, one more medieval *Annunciation*, with the Holy Spirit as white dove, beaming god's seed through the blessed eardrum, so the holy hymen remains intact. A laser blue, not on the Virgin's cloak but in the ray streaming from the dove. Today the ghost of that remote blue signal haunts him, buzzing in his bad ear as he climbs the stair to the third floor on the Dvortsovaya side.

He meant to go straight to the Matisse room, but got lost. The Hermitage is new to him; this is his second day. From the look of *her* she lives here; she has that red-gold look that he tells himself crops up frequently in Slavs. Not that he caught more than a sidelong glance yesterday. It was her manner, patient, even slightly bored, in a proprietorial way, that said: We wish to be alone, leave us. And the minders did.

Zach hurries through the Picasso room without stopping to look at the pictures he missed yesterday. He enters the room of waiting and –

there she is!

Or is she?

Is that yesterday's woman? She is sitting in the same room but something's not right. For one thing she's wearing blue, not black, but that's neither here nor there. He's changed too, into something black. Today she's wearing a kind of soft acrylic tracksuit, powder-blue, and pink bobby socks with little furry pompoms that hang like cowbells over the back of white runners. He imagines them ringing as she runs.

But her hair is red, the same red, and her posture has not changed, leaning forward with her chin in her hand.

>There, as Zach comes up behind her, is the window in her back, the same high pink skin with its peach-fuzz nap that ripens into red-gold down.

>There is the same vertiginous fold where the flesh gullies.

>And there is the same red line of lace.

And yet something has changed. True, she still looks as if she'd like to go closer to the painting, and even touch if there were no alarm bells and cameras, but the aura of belonging, of living here in these quarters, once home to the Tsarina's ladies-in-waiting, has vanished. This body says: *Look, I run ten miles every morning and feel the better for it and I think you should too but don't get me wrong, I'm an artist.*

Zach, who is an artist in his own way, or what's he doing here, is immediately on his guard. But, but, but, there's the small matter of that line of red lace. What's it doing *there*? Because the tracksuit seems expressly chosen, that shade of blue, to dampen any ardour in the onlooker and possibly in the wearer too. It's not exactly Virgin Mary blue but nor is it water-nymph aqua, or odalisque turquoise, or even a crackling protopunk electric blue. It's by no means that bacchanalian midnight blue that verges on purple, nor a savage sadomasochistic bruised-eye indigo, and it's a long way from the gentian violet of the orgiast.

No. It's a straight-out daytime sky blue, bland as a button.

So what's the red flag for? Because it's no common red. It's a snatch-and-grab red that turns the lunge into a wicked finger working the seam where you divide. This red bays at you from depths where light bends back on itself and the spectrum warps to a sub-violet beyond colour.

Zach stares helplessly through the window like a prisoner who, after years in his cell, finds there are no bars. Rubbing his eyes, he climbs through the ellipse, builds a hut under that flesh-tinted sky and dwells an eternity on the downy red-gold meadow, looking out across the snap-brim of blue sea. At nightfall he stares up from the freckled cornfields, turning to whistle after his sheepdog who's gone nosing down the path to where a stream of drawn light from the evening star pours endlessly down the forbidden cleft.

The woman turns and notices him there and stands up to make way, in the courteous manner of seasoned gallery-goers whose dance has instinctive rules, the leaning away, the stepping aside, the moving on, the circling return. It's this action that convinces Zach he's wrong about her. Yesterday's woman was outside all rules, in her own dimension, where politeness and civility and sociability have no meaning.

'It's almost creepy.'

She's spoken, to him.

She nods at the picture as she moves off. 'He never trusted blue.'

Right off he can think of nothing to say. It doesn't register until she's gone that she means the sinister triffid pattern of the tablecloth, the arabesques crawling towards the maid in black, and swarming up the wall.

American, he registers next, and can place the accent precisely, Midwest, because he was once there himself. Four scholarship years studying music in Ohio. Suddenly the socks, the tracksuit, the runners, fall into place. *Baby* blue, that past delivers a free refinement, at the opposite end of the universe from the laser blue of the Virgin. Russian, he'd assumed she was yesterday, because of where they are. And because of the arctic flush in the window on her back.

But what was she wearing then? Now he can't be sure. Already the present is erasing the past.

She's waiting for him in the Picasso room next door. A new look on her alert face that says: *You know, if this guy were not so good you could find it in your heart to dislike him.* But distanced, ironic; the devout glow of the Matisse room is gone. Again, yesterday's woman had a sullen, slightly pouty, dreamy look, not this bright American poise.

'*Look* at this, I mean. You'd think he was terrified of colour. All these cubist guys set the tone – black, white, grey – for half a century. Photographers are still scared witless of colour and here is where it started. And of course the avant garde loved him. The Steins – you know the Steins?'

Zach does but her tone says she doesn't really expect him to or care particularly if he does; this could be a Platonic dialogue conducted in her head with him as virtual referee. Besides he's not a talker.

'The Steins bought Matisse to start with, then decided Picasso was the future. Because he broke all the rules – what Gertrude would do to language. Because all she could see, all anyone could see, was line. The line on the page, the line on the canvas. We think of the modernist revolution as one of broken form, right? So who's the hero? The guy who breaks line, breaks noses. *This* guy. But lookit.'

She walks him back to the doorway from where they can see *The Red Room* hanging in the distance.

'He's worked that trick already, Gert. Red did it. Colour did it, not mirrors.'

Meres. Buckeye? Hawkeye? Hoosier? Great Lakes, anyway. Somewhere around 1790, the Virginians are pushing back the Shawnee and this sound is born into the hive.

'And not lines. Just a faint line there, see – a red line – between the red table and the red wall. Even his lines are colours. Red just broke all the rules and bedded down with red. But I guess line won in the end – *this* guy. Line is mind, right? Brain. Colour is animal stuff, just matter. Light.'

She can't just stand there; she's drawn back, and draws him back, to the other room.

'You know what this was at first?' They're standing in front of the picture where they started. '*The* Blue *Room*. If you look at it in a colour negative it still is.'

She can't help it, oral to her epiglottis she wants to share it with him. The other one – he's sure now it was another woman

– looked like she'd swallow the picture whole and never show it to anyone; it was *hers*. Her private property.

'You know how all these paintings ended up here, in Petersburg?'

'No.'

'A couple of Russian tycoons just went to these guys' studios in Paris and bought stuff right off the easel. Shchukin and Morozov. They liked it so much they had standing orders from Moscow. And just when they were finished hanging them in their houses the revolution broke out and – *voilà* – suddenly all this belonged to the people.'

'Thank God for that.'

'*Beelzebub*,' she corrects him, leaning towards him, then decides he doesn't know the song, so sings a line. '*Pleased to meet you, I hope you know my name.* You're too young for the Stones.'

Zach looks at her, offended. The other one was younger too. So how old *are* you exactly? Aunty, maybe, he decides, not Mom. He sings, distinctly, taking her key by way of proof: '*Was it your* aunty, *your* uncle? *Now –* '

'*WHO'S BEEN SLEEPING HERE?*' they burst into the chorus together and laugh out loud.

The ice is broken, but so is her thread.

'What was I saying?' she wants to know, when they've recovered.

'And saying,' he risks.

She twists a lip and hangs her head and looks up from under a line of red. Feels the warm breath of complicity so turns him around by the shoulders to face the other way and propels him, he could be her nephew, or something, towards the painting on the opposite wall.

'OK. Look at this.'

It's a shock. What shakes him so his jaw drops is that yesterday's woman is standing there, looking at him. From the painting. She's in the goddamn painting. *Gaadamn*. (Four years at Dorian, Ohio, he can't say it any other way.)

'Are you married? No? Here is married life for you, here's what's in store. This is *The Painter's Family*. Madame Matisse on the sofa knitting, her boys Pierre and whatsisname playing checkers, and Matisse's daughter by another woman standing here, a little apart, with her book of poetry.'

Zach stands up, fronts the painting conscientiously, like Maximilian facing the firing squad. He has a scrupulous way of lifting his eyebrows into the emblem *Looking*, as if the eye needs a special dispensation in a man of the ear. A good listener, as she's divined, how good she can't yet know.

He avoids the young woman's gaze, looking at every point except her. The painting imposes a high vantage, so the Moroccan rug, which dominates the lower half, shows almost in plan. No windows here, a pure interior, yet it's a brighter canvas than the other. No horizon either: wall and floor meet in a seamless plane of floral paper and patterned rug and wildly maculate upholstery. In the centre, a fireplace – this is the domestic hearth in a family gathering. But the key member in this family is missing. On the mantelshelf is his stand-in, a sculpture by Matisse himself called (its name is significant in a picture of domestic leisure) *The Serf*. Matisse worked hard at painting, and could go on about it.

'The fire is out,' she points at the black fireplace. 'But he's lit it in the room.'

The boys wear blazing red suits even as they doze over their game. In later life Pierre will recall the tedium of these sittings;

16

the painting shows Matisse knows how they felt. With a few crisp brush strokes this colourist with line catches the moods of his sitters: boredom in the boys, abstraction in his wife, and in his fifteen-year-old daughter, on the edge of womanhood, a molten mix of emotions as she, and only she, gazes out of the painting. She wears a sombre black dress (unlike the red in a portrait of her at ten, reading) while at the other end of the room Madame Matisse's ochre gown is splashed with yellow flowers. Light, pattern, space, flood the painting.

'It's all surface, right?'

'I guess.' You slip back into the old tongue, he thinks. Then: she's right, the painting clarifies looked at her way. Then: she's wearing green shoes, the girl in the painting. Something weird about her, though. He forces himself to look up, runs his eye up the black sweep of her dress past the white lace collar, and yes, she's still looking at him. Or, more unnerving, just over his shoulder, with a steely smile. It's her all right.

He turns to the flesh and blood woman beside him, small, slight. Lanky himself, with mutinous black hair cropped by an army pensioner.

'That wasn't you yesterday?'

'What wasn't?'

'In here. Staring at that other painting.'

'I just got here today.'

He accepts that but needs a break now. He waves at a window. 'Can we get a bit of fresh air?'

'Why not?'

She studies him for the first time. Armenian, she thinks, with that nose, or Aramaic. Jesus without the beard in AD 35, two years into Kashmir: still mercurial, but morose, gentling into obscurity.

Her eyes drop to his fingers, two octaves from tip to tip. He's waggling them in the air, all four straight out, shaking a make-believe hand.

'Zach,' he says. 'Zaccheus, not Zachariah. Not all Indians are called Ram and Rahim.'

She smiles and places all five fingertips of one hand on her chest.

'Aline. Not Aileen.'

PART 2

The Abecedary A–Z

A *is for* A line

See also A ppendix

A line

Zach and Aline ride the elevator down and step out on the square between the giant Atlas feet of the entrance. A penny drops. He looks at her.

'You got here today and already you're at the Hermitage?'

She smiles acknowledgement. 'A disciple. I came straight here off the plane.'

'Just the one master?'

'Just the one master. And you? What brings you here?'

'A festival. They're celebrating their 300th anniversary, the city. Petersburg. Music is one of the events.'

'And?'

'I got invited.'

'What sort of music?' She means him, his.

He opens his mouth and finds it closing without saying anything. That happens when he's pressed for a definition of what he does.

'New,' he decides. 'Contemporary ... it has various labels. Serious, which is sadly true. I'm part of the celebrations.'

'So, you're famous?'

'No, just lucky. They needed some tan among the whites and yellows.'

'But you have works, opuses? Opiiii?'

'It helps.'

'Amazing!'

'Hardly.'

'Well, not amazing. Remarkable.'

'That helped too. We're supposed to improvise, down there. Like your Africans. I stick out at home too. I got rhythm. But I'm not complaining: maybe it got me here.'

'Come on, don't give me that token stuff.'

'It's true. I was trawling the Net and I came across their calendar. There's other stuff too, jugglers and so on. It's a big festival. I will say they look after you.'

'Like, you're not on bread and water.'

'No, it's nice to be coddled.'

'Where?'

'The Hilton.'

'Hilton! Bound hand and foot, eh?'

Zach grins. 'Try it sometime.'

They walk in silence a minute, Zach breathing in the temperate air, Aline beating a distracted air with her middle finger on the rail of the canal. They cross the Griboedova by the Bank Bridge, Zach pats the paws of a gold-winged griffin, sniffs sharp, taking it all in. He feels a draught of boredom creep from her, or it could be impatience, so turns to face her.

'How do you like it?' He means it all, everything, and lifts both arms to include all Petersburg, on this her first day.

'Peter? Well, it's not Paris.'

'Why should it be?'

Chid, she thinks for a bit. 'You didn't grow up in Chillicothe.'

'You didn't grow up in the *Doon*.'

'Where's that?'

'Exactly.'

'Then you know about Dullsville.'

'Intimately.'

'And you like it there.'

It's his turn to think. 'It gives places like this their tang. But also you love it for its own sake,' he adds on reflection. 'Mostly for its own sake.'

'Which is what?'

Stumped, he prevaricates. 'If you can put a finger on it it's probably wrong. It's just, what, home? Places like this give *it* its tang.'

'Take your word for it.'

'I mean, this is nice, but can you imagine *living* here?'

'Better here than Chillicothe.'

'But why!'

'You go there some day.'

'I've been next door. I lived four years in Cooper's Creek.'

'Cooper's *Creek*! And lived to tell the tale.'

'And almost went native.'

'You're not kidding.'

'No. Part of me is still there.' He glances up the canal as if it might still be visible on the horizon.

'Piece of the heart?'

'You could say.' He turns back as the vignette, and the face in it, fades. 'It almost became home.'

'You'd have lasted ten seconds, honeychile. *Long* seconds.'

'I'd have lasted,' he lowers his eyes, 'as long as it took.'

Wednesday's child, she thinks, woe his birthright. She drops her gaze too, ready for the first time to believe he exists. He sees the mask working loose.

'I could live here,' she confesses. 'I *do* live here half the year.'

'I thought you just got here?'

'Just got *back* here.'

'Ah. Like the tern.'

'Yeah, turn, turn, turn. But winter here and summer there.'

'*Winter* here! No thanks. Where's summer?'

'New York.'

'Ah. SoHo loft.'

'Not really.'

She won't say she has a roof garden with a 280-degree view.

'And here?'

'We're there.' She nods at the mews behind the griffins. 'Show you.'

We're there. He can't tell which is the operative word. The sentence tilts back and forth crazily. But there's a new glow to the griffins, whose wings come to a point at the perpendicular. They're her black leopards, on gold chains, and suddenly they're smiling.

She leads the way through the old carriage arch whose haunches on either side bear a medallion set in a plaster roundel. The same griffins rampant, less friendly. He trips on a cobblestone and finds his footing nimbly; kicks the stone back, a heel grind with mock malice as if to send it through to the other end of the earth.

'That's always a stumbling block,' she laughs.

'*Always?*'

26

'It got me too, the first time.'

Her laugh tinkles like a fallen ring in the sandstone arena they've entered, a small stone quad with a bent cherry in one corner and a golden elm in the middle. At the cherry is a staircase that climbs steeply behind a security gate of half-inch wrought iron. *Aline Medlar* says the brass plate. She inserts a card in a satin-steel slot and the gate rolls open. It clangs shut behind them as they climb. The stair turns at right angles again and again; they're in some kind of turret. Three landings up it stops at a single door: her staircase, her turret. Another stainless-steel slot, another card or the same.

Chaos inside the apartment, right up to the door, like the place has been ransacked. Clothes lie in drifts on the furniture, on the floor; files, stacks of photographs, catalogues, newspapers in various stages of consumption, magazines with a coffee mug as a paperweight, a half-eaten beansprout sandwich on a plate, sprouting.

'No, the KGB haven't been,' she acknowledges his look. 'Not lately.'

It's a long narrow apartment or series of apartments strung into one, the old partitions broken through so what was once a series of private views is now a bank of windows looking onto the canal. The midday sun streams in, making a series of blinding lozenges, one for each fanlight, along the blond parquet. He looks out of the nearest window and yes, there are her griffins, keeping watch. She watches him walk the length of the corridor, at home, and admires the ease of it yet finds it minutely disquieting. She's busy picking up coffee mugs, finds a muffin mouldering in a *Herald Tribune* wigwam. *Feb*ruary, Jesus! She won't let cleaners in, won't let anybody.

'So *this* is your loft,' he says returning. He likes the echo of a wood floor. At home they're terrazzo and silent.

'Loft's upstairs. We'll go there,' she says, in no hurry. She takes all the newspapers and makes a bale that she drops down a chute in the kitchen wall. 'Shit, that clogs it,' she remembers too late, and punches a red button beside the hatch.

'The piano didn't come up the stairs,' he says, and nods down the corridor. The kitchen is the third in the series of rooms after the lounge. There must be twenty beyond it.

'That. There's a service elevator at the other end of the building. Of course you play.'

'Strictly theory.' When he must lie he shakes his head diagonally.

'I don't even have that, but it looks nice, and it was a bargain in Antwerp.'

The rest of the mess she leaves and makes coffee; black, sugarless without asking. 'The thing you respect most about him,' she says and he knows by the way she puts his mug down on the floor beside the beanbag, deliberately, elastically, she means the Master, 'is he's always arguing but he never paints a thesis. You remember the rug in the painting? All the spots dancing? It's the same in every painting. Every spot counts. If there's a yard with a pink tree and a yellow tree, he'll treat the brown paving like it's the main clause, not an afterthought. And the same with the grey kerb and the same with the green drain and the same with the black drainhole. They all have equal weight.'

'*All* main clauses?'

'Well, maybe not,' she smiles, 'but each gets the same attention. Like in life. I mean, nothing nothing *nothing* is *really* more important than anything else, right?'

Red

'But red is more equal?' He's going by the curtains now.

'Red is more equal,' she laughs. 'Unfortunately that's also how a decorator works and it's one of the things people always held against him: Matisse the colourist who ducks the ugliness. Prettifies. Matisse the bourgeois. But look, he's done his time in bohemia, lived cheap, fathered a daughter on a model, and now for the first time, thanks to Shchukin, he's making a bit of money. He's not complaining, he's showing his father he's not a total dummy. He can buy a house. He's a bourgeois and he knows it: it's the *other* guys who are busy pretending to be something else.

'Every morning he makes himself a pot of chocolate and disappears into the garden shed and goes to work. On light. Mixes a little yellow ochre and applies it. Sits there staring into space, working. Like a shepherd or a street-corner man, loitering with intent. And he starts to see things. Ochre next to indigo makes a hole in space like acid. A dab of grey alongside deepens it, sets an echo going right down at the bottom, and then just one straw of Naples yellow smuggled in there – and he's tunnelled out into some other dimension.

'You don't see it till you cut the canvas into ribbons, and read one band across or down. It's like one of those Moebius strips that loops back and back into 1907, Tuesday morning so many seconds past ten past the table with the goldfish bowl over the plum tree and through the willow between the last catkin and the cloud that's changing from an aardvark into something else.'

A*ar*dv*ar*k, not one but two delicious *r*s. Z takes one step back. There's a tunnel at his feet he could drop straight down if he's not careful, bright steel with rifling so he'd go spinning, heaven light at the far end and honey in the mouth.

'Show you.'

She gets up, checks his mug for coffee, still some, and goes running lightly down the corridor into one of the farther rooms, bare feet, nails unpainted like the nails on her hands. Comes back with a scrolled canvas and a pair of scissors and a pillbox.

'You ever done Velox?'

'Not now.'

He means not this week, not while he's here on show.

'Come on.'

She twists off the lid and carefully shakes a pill into her own mug then hangs the box over the rim of his. He lifts one hand, she sees the index finger part from the rest and tilts a fraction further till a small white pill slips over the edge.

'This,' she unrolls the canvas, 'is the Master.'

Zach stares. It's not a print. Not a poster. It's canvas, not paper. Already the paint has cracks in it, not old-master cracks, just cracks. High Modern cracks.

'Drink up.'

He hesitates, then lifts the mug and downs it in one go. She does the same and spreads the canvas on the floor between them, sliding back along the parquet like a chess queen as the painting unrolls.

'This is something called *Aloes in the Cemetery at St Honorat*. He actually did some of it out in the open but then covered it up with another view of the same trees from a window. I had it X-rayed. If we cut like so' – she cuts a narrow strip along the top, a finger's width, maybe less – 'we get to see as he saw: not what he saw but how he saw.'

She turns the corner and pauses, the scissors jaws open. 'Hold your end and pull tight. Harder.'

She starts to cut again, finds the sweet point on the blades, a

30

furrow between two threads, then glides the open scissors, a strip of canvas peeling off as she goes. Again and again, the canvas dwindling to a core. Zach gawps.

'*Now* look.' She pulls a stretch lamp down, already reading the strip in her hands.

He sees a ribbon of dots and dashes, like old Morse code.

'You see the way this gold sits beside this blue, what it's doing? See the back and forth? The way they feed each other. Tell on each other, kiss and make up? Or this blue and this kind of pistachio. See the way the brush falls, see the stroke coming down and then pushing into the blue, see how it nudges. Go closer, hold it up against the light. See?'

He's seeing as never before. She fetches a magnifying glass and he sees the room swell and dissolve in its luminous circle. Mottled brown and violet swim under his eye like cold-water fish, then a tangerine so upsetting he leans over and falls in without a splash, hangs there underwater, a waterbaby sucking on mutant lungs, on tadpole eyes. The brushstrokes come up close and nibble, he strokes their sides and watches them flick away, heliotrope with umber, scales of colour whose logic he now begins dimly to perceive. Watches them knit together and come apart, is there at the moment of their birth, presides over their dissolution.

'You're not afraid of beauty, are you, Zach?'

He is, always was. Distrustful of the mute appeal of a red scarf fallen on a black-tile floor. Of two notes – let alone three – agreeing sweetly.

'Like all those lousy Chelsea gallerists. I mean you don't *really* believe all that crapola about rupture? Do you, Zach?'

He does, or did. He wrote *Ashwamedha* and twenty other

pieces with a pencil Dorian made sure was sharpened to a cruel point. Aleatory progression, serious silence, theory, theory, till he came to believe. But this cutting up she's done; doesn't it smell a little bit of theory, fractal intervention or some such thing? He lowers the magnifying glass and turns to the sorry remains of the canvas.

She reads the look. 'Don't fret. He'd have approved. He was a scissors and paste man. Well, he'd have approved in theory. But probably he'd be madder'n hell!' She's laughing.

'With disciples like you, who needs Judas?'

'It's just a copy. They do some incredible fakes in this town. Everyone, students, professionals, technicians. This is the city of the Hermitage, don't forget.'

Now he feels cheated and she reads that too.

'OK, it's real, it *was*. I bought it, or my husband did. It was the real *Aloes*. But we didn't destroy it, we set it free. When Matisse went to visit Shchukin in Moscow he threw a fit because his *Music* was behind glass. Shchukin reminded him the musicians already lived in a frame, so what was a bit of glazing? But there *are* paintings where cutups don't work. Come on upstairs.'

She's on her feet, from cross-legged to standing in a scissors movement that has him revising her age. He stands up, his head so light every hair on it has found an independent tangent. His eyes so heavy they could spin off into space and find new orbits. His body newly moulted, the old skin in a heap on the floor, feet oddly sure as he follows her heels up a vertical face.

Up above is a blank white wall, the same that holds the ladder he's on with four steel pins, and a plasma screen. He holds on tight, afraid of falling. Ladders at home he leaves to painters, house painters, and he could be a mile up this one. More. The floor looks like earth from space. He looks for the Great Wall of China. The screen is downloading something.

'It's the *Red Studio*. From 1911.'

It's a window but when she opens it the painting's still hanging there. The window frame, the sill, lead nowhere else. There is only the painting. Scandal-red and still pitching at the speed of light. He's ravished, blown away.

'We can go in, but you have to do as I say, all right? You can't touch anything in there.' She takes his hand. 'Except me.'

'OK.'

It's all red. The whole thing, every wall, floor and ceiling, down to the furniture. A new red. Yellow in it, but the reddest red he's seen.

Something strange has happened to the hand that's leading him. It's gone behind glass and been refracted. It's gone specimen flat and the lines and bones stand out in white, as if she's entered a special kind of outsize X-ray chamber. Her head too has flattened out, and the rest of her, like a figure from an Egyptian mural. It's so foreign he should by rights have a visa. He looks down, his mouth suddenly dry with wanting her, and finds he's going like that too. The room is a bagatelle, the furniture all pins and string.

'Ah-ah, don't touch, remember. This is where he worked. Works. This is 1911. That nude in the corner no longer exists in your time, our time, it was destroyed.'

The table nearest them, which has a wineglass and a painted dish and a vase of nasturtiums, has stood up, turned into geometry. If the still life things on it had bulk to them they'd slide straight off. She hops onto it and stays all the same.

'*OK*,' she says, sitting there, her voice gone italicized and coming from all sides so it surrounds him like a gas. *'Do as I say?'*

He nods. Standing right there at the table looking into her eyes.

She holds up her hands. *'Paint me.'*

She picked the idea clean out of his brain: he wants that more than anything. Just the sight of her mouth like a crushed rose, her unsocked feet, makes him want to strip and paint her, smother her in something if not himself. There's only the tracksuit to take off but his hands are shaking from the wave of need that swamps him leaving only his mouth dry. The red line of lace from the Hermitage is invisible against the skin of her that's gone red like everything in the studio. When she's naked, her clothes stick flat on the wall. Like the clothes of a princess spread on the banks of a stream in an old miniature. She lies back on the tabletop into no depth. To keep her there he'd have to tie her down, he thinks, if gravity still applied. And paint her some other colour or she'd disappear in the universal red.

She reaches back and hands him a spray can. He squirts a puff into the general air, testing. It hangs there at eye level in a barren brilliant cloud, silver-grey.

He paints her from the feet up, watching intently as first the nails then the toes go metallic. Her feet are silverfish, her thighs tinfoil, the bush steel wool. The face must be done top down, the hair on the head in one light circling swoop. While the paint dries he inspects the ochre frames, the pottery, the sculpture; she studies the grandfather clock without hands.

'All right,' she says, in that same papery mica membrane voice and turns and sweeps the table clear. Dish and vase and wine glass go floating through the red void to new locations. *'Now,'*

she turns to him and spreads her arms. He unfolds her like a wall chart cunningly hidden in the back of an old abecedary and pins her to the table.

A is for A line. She looks up at him.

'Kill me.'

A ppendix

The seed merchant's son is in bed
henri with his appendix
vermiform   inflamed there
still small m matisse eighteen he
stares at the lines on his hand   he has tried
he's studied the law   stuck one toe in that turbid water
mornings he climbed eight flights of steps no sweat
to learn design   he fingers the curtains
last year he thought to turn apothecary
this year he needs the medicine
his mother enters playing Pandora
sets a paintbox in his lap   on the blanket
stands back to watch the wrapper coming off
the catch resisting deliciously   then lifting
off the gold nipple   lid coming up   on glory
twenty billion   billion   permutations spring out
the future unformed but seen whole   for one
nanosecond   and already he's curing
he'll spit on academicians' top hats from above
lob glue pellets at the bouquinistes on the quai
terrorize the century mildly from his studio
end of the nameless placeless bellyache
end of black   doubt
start of red
song

B *is for* Blackshorts

Blackshorts

Nag dips a fingertip in mustard oil and strokes the mound of lampblack in the basin. He shuts his eyes, mutters a mantra, and draws the sign of the king cobra on his forehead: a ring that loops down to the bridge of the nose in the middle and doubles back up to end in another ring. In black it's the negative of the white spectacles the cobra carries on its hood, a mark little boys throughout the land leave regularly in the dust when they first discover that the addition of a short horizontal transforms the ancient symbol into a cock-and-balls.

Immediately he swipes sideways smudging the mock caste-mark.

One of his eyelids droops, a tic gone stuck, so half his face looks alert and the other half sleepy. The division has worked its way into his brain, or has sprung from there, making for a man seemingly at war with himself. He is sometimes remote and sometimes confiding, by turns mild and savage. Nobody in the gang knows how to read his face and this is his strength. Right or left, you might approach him from the wrong side. He is not young but his hair is thick and black and he might be vain of it but for the flared ears it fails to conceal. Here too a defect works in his favour: he appears to be listening in, so the others are careful of what they say, except maybe Gilgitan.

Next he dips all the fingers together and blacks his temples left and right, cheeks left and right, and chin. The ears he blacks diligently. Earlobes, jawline, and neck complete the sanctum. The remainder is less carefully done: chest, upper arms, lower, back of right hand. Belly, a round rub that skirts the navel, down to the band of the black shorts, then the front of the thighs, hams, shins, ankles. Lastly: elbows, a finical touch, like a libertine applying cologne, left and right. Left before right in everything. The little finger of the left hand is left unblacked.

His Snakeship is ready.

The others follow, smearing, dipping, patting by the light of the kerosene lamp. Making snakes of themselves. The youngest uses a little shaving mirror to the amusement of the rest; he has stood it on the floor before him like an easel and works with concentration, stretching out his legs first one then the other, disregarding the jibes that fill the unfurnished room. He has peeled off his soft T-shirt that says CORTO MALTESE (he can read that, but what does it mean and who's the handsome soldier?). Not yet thirty, he is already going bald at the crown and on either side of a tuft in the front, but that doesn't stop the girls from looking at him. At the back of the head the hair is thick and spiky like a comb. Lean, shrewd, and resourceful, Gilgitan took no time at all to switch to the left hand for eating; they eat that way when the gang is alone together. The others secretly envy his self-possession.

Except for Gilgitan, who must eat to perform, the rest have eaten nothing. Nothing is taken before a smudge, not even liquor for courage. Afterwards there will be grog and weed and meat. Come drunk and you are debarred.

RED

When all are ready Phuljari, oldest among them, he might be fifty, lifts the oil lamp to a niche in the wall beside the goddess. He is so dark-skinned the blacking hardly shows on him; as if in recognition of this his application is the sketchiest of the lot. The others never forget to chivvy him and he stretches his thin purple lips in a continuous smile during the operation, but once the sooting is done he turns solemn and officious and hides his buck teeth. His wall eye simply means the good one's twice as sharp; once it saved him when the night-patrol cops took him for an idiot.

The goddess is Nagouri, the village protectress. Her idol is painted white in the forest shrine in a small clearing among the young sal trees, her worship confused with the worship of a beauty who died young ninety years ago; here she is dark. In this niche she is recognizable by her symbol, the banana tree, which she is said to favour; she holds a different edged weapon in three hands and a banana-flower stem, rigid and swollen at the tip, in the fourth. Beside her hangs a framed oleograph of Kali doing her frenzied dance of the severed heads. According to local tradition Nagouri cut off her own head and held it out to the grisly Mother as an offering to save the village from being swept away in a flash flood. The Mother took the head from the first passing creature and placed it back on her neck. The creature happened to be a cobra and Nagouri lived to produce a hooded child a fortnight for a whole year till she died.

Gilgitan, former truck painter and occasional niche painter, did her for a bottle of rum for the owner of this house, Paltaniya, a sometime corporal who now has a cotton-carding business. Born to blackshorts, Paltaniya steered clear of them during his army career, but has backslid in retirement. His pucca house is open to

41

the fraternity on nights such as this but he is too old now to accompany them on their expeditions. He will stay up cooking thirtysixchilli pork till they return. He is in the front room, unblacked and keeping watch. He will keep the goddess company.

The men prostrate themselves before her one by one, first Nag, then wall-eyed Phuljari, then Vinod and Chhanga, twins in every respect except Vinod doesn't have six fingers on each hand. Lastly Gilgitan, who turns his action into press-ups when he's done. In this position he looks extraordinarily like the wiry garden lizard of his nickname. He is still trembling from a job done this afternoon in a killing hut in the middle of nowhere. Ordinarily he would have saved his energy for this night but he's had the pig girl on his mind lately. He's just come from the slaughter, and stopped by her house to let her know the big bruiser is no more. His shoulder is grazed where the boar dragged him before the knife went in, him and another man, clear across the floor of the shed and around and around, smashing them up against the walls. He has splashes of dry blood in his hair, pigsqueal stuck in his ear. Now he sits cross-legged with the rest and shuts his eyes tight and pinches the bridge of his nose like them and recites the doxology they have learnt since they came of age:

> *You look after your own.*
> *You hold the world in your palm*
> *You have no rival*
> *Nothing is owned except by you*
> *Your red tongue would slice me in two*
> *Your eyes fry me*
> *I hear your dance in my blood*
> *Spare me this night.*

They tug on their earlobes for a moment, then turn their backs on her as they leave the room, left foot first.

At the front door Paltaniya takes leave of them with a mock military salute and they slip away into the shadows towards the riverbed. Their forefathers wore a codpiece instead of shorts. They carry no weapons, for that would make them dacoits, five or more armed men, and dacoitee carries a harsher sentence. But each has knotted about his wrist a piece of gut string that will quiet a noisy homeowner.

Softly they go.

Chalk dust of stars. Night black as a queen.

C *is for* C ybercafe

See also C offee, *C omposeur,*
    C omputer

C ybercafe

Mrs Goyal, proprietor of the Goyal Cybercafe-cum-Lending Library, sits on a gold chariot.

One of twenty on the cheap blockprint cloth spread over the bed set along a wall of the narrow glass-fronted shop. This is the library wall. Above her oiled bun are three shelves of paperbacks showing trussed-up women and bloodstained knives. The other wall is the cyber wall, five cubicles, each with a computer and a curtain rail but no curtains. (The curtains were removed after the Goyals found the privacy was being misused.) Mrs Goyal was not always the proprietor of a cybercafe. Her husband, whose garlanded photo hangs on the third wall, facing you as you enter, once ran a grocery shop in this very space. The fourth wall is glass, on the street. Secretly Mrs Goyal regards those early years with contempt; a lending library is a step up from flour and sugar, but a *cybercafe* is very heaven. Just before he died Mr Goyal bought five decrepit computers for nothing and had a carpenter make five plywood tables with partitions. With his provident fund Mrs Goyal added the glass front that makes of this room an oven.

Apart from the enlarged photo of the late Mr Goyal, garlanded with withered marigolds and speared with incense sticks, there is a calendar showing a boychild in the hood shade of a hundred-headed cobra, and a door leading to the living quarters. But this is clearly the living room. Leaned up against a shiny patch of limewash Mrs Goyal reads a local paper, now looking up at the row of websurfers along the opposite wall, now staring out at the traffic of the busy Haridwar Road through the sheet glass of the shopfront with the words GOYAL CYBERCAFE CUM LENDING LIBRARY painted in red there. From the inside the words appear backwards and she often runs her eyes along the doubly unfamiliar characters.

As I wait my turn at the glass door a pimply goatish boy in the first cubicle has one eye on Mrs Goyal as he clicks between tabs on the taskbar. Every time she looks down he clicks back to a pair of melon-sized breasts stored in a computer in Texas.

The boy has a loosened blue-and-old-gold school tie around his scrawny neck; over his open collar spills a pair of furred wattles. He strokes one with his right hand, the absent-minded stroke of a practised stroker. He could be me from forty years ago, but this minute I'm too hot for sentiment. I have a story to tell. Two stories, you will have noticed, red and black like the wires positive and negative in a cable.

1. Red: Aline and Zach, in Petersburg
2. Black: Gilgitan of the blackshorts, here in Dariya Dun

Insulated from each other, for now, but let them touch naked and o my lord the fireworks. There's a third story too, my own, you could call it the earth wire, Green. Keep an eye on all three while I watch the boy. He has to keep an eye on the clock too. When his time is up he pays and leaves in a hurry, looking drawn and spent.

I (call me N) slip into the newly vacated cubicle. The seat is unpleasantly warm. The keyboard is worn smooth and somebody has scratched the vanished letters on each key with the point of a divider. My knees are jammed up against the table, my back against the glass with the shop name. It is thirty-nine degrees centigrade and there is one fan distributing the hot air. I type in my password and for the next forty-five minutes attend to my email, losing two messages to bad connectivity along the way. At the end of an hour I'm waiting only for a sent message confirmation. It can take ten minutes. It can take forever.

At the crossroads outside is a urinal with three men using it, two looking up at a dripping Bipasha Basu in a poster for the newest movie hit, *Jism*. I know how they feel; she makes a jelly of me too. But it's now forty degrees centigrade, well past jelly, and as the sweat pours off me I'm ready to scream. Not only has the sent message confirmation failed to appear, my painstakingly typed message has simply vanished into space. My knees have locked. I am fifty-one years old, not fifteen. What am I doing here?

There is something sticky on the floor under my shoe and it's not chewing gum. It's – o my god.

Right. That's it.

That's it. (I type in large

letters and leave it on the screen for the next customer to see.)

I will arise now and go ... free never again never never never never will I darken these filthy doors

ever

I will buy me a C omputer
And go on the Net
On the World Wide Web

And I did.

C omputer

Elementary. But why did I, no pauper, no Luddite, wait ten years to go online?

One man stood in the way. Dilavar Singh, lineman. Line-tapper, line-fixer, line-shifter. With the Net your connectivity is only as good as your phone line, and if the line is being farmed out to someone else for weeks at a time (once it was months) what good is the speed of light? With a little help from Dilavar Singh, a bottle merchant got to share my number – the lineman simply unplugged me at the pole and plugged him in.

Never mind the Net: why have a phone? Days when I could have ripped the line out of the wall I quietly paid the bills – bills on a dead phone – because there was a queue six years long for a telephone. And you queued up to pay, too, month after month, waiting for it to come right.

And now it has. The mobile phone is here, is everywhere, and it has the linemen of this town running scared. Not just one company, several to pick from. People are switching over, and if Dilavar Singh doesn't shape up the landline will become extinct – and with it his job. (And with it, god is good, Dilavar Singh.)

At last a home computer makes sense. I still have the landline, but the balance of power has shifted.

Of course connectivity varies at home too. But you're at home, not at Mrs Goyal's.

Email:

To: Zaccheus Wilding
Subject: ONLINE!

>*Young Z*

Where does this come to you from? One guess.

No, not a cybercafe. One more go. Whose machine is this?

Yes!

At home.

Why have I waited all these years? Scumbag Dilavar Singh is a paper tiger.

Can you imagine, can you REALLY imagine, how hard it is to switch from a fountain pen after writing four million words?

It's easy.

And if the flat screen is beautiful – just beautiful – it's sinfully pleasurable.

Save me.

N

But next, C for Confession, for Curiosity, I sent another email, briefer and yet fuller. I had no intention of sending until Chance turned up a certain New York address. Of an alphabet closer to me than Z, and yet further than any other. O. The Chicana. The ex.

RED

To: Olivia.Gutierrez@yOGabydancing.com

> *O*
> *>Flourishing?*
> *Just wondering.*
> *And Mandalay?*
> *What's six years?*
> *N*
> *(Ministry of Bolts from the Blue)*

Came the reply:

> *N*
> *>What are you after? There are laws in this country. She's
> just fine and not at all like you. So, I'm not the Queen of
> Diamonds, I'm my own boss. Managing without men. Saw a
> book of yours in B&N remainder pile so had to buy it, but you
> know I don't read novels. Manda reckons she's read enough
> books too, hates school. But can she sing! Said the other
> day she's old enough to travel alone, meaning I don't know
> what. Maybe she has your mouth, I hope not your other
> appetites. Where's the poor camellia now?*
> *O*

Note the indent. She rubs in what our initials spell out: NO.
The celebrated NON of Matisse's blue *Conversation*, which shows
the artist and his wife squaring off, could not be more succinct –
compare my upbeat ON – but do I know my woman? Herewith a
line gloss:

I am *after*, was after, nothing.

I invoked no *laws*, simply gave up custody.

She is not *like* me, I know, she's like her mother, beautiful. The mother full-fleshed, one of Piero's heavier angels (but dark-haired), that severe but succulent beauty that used to be called statuesque, with yOGa and tofu to keep the dogs of fat leashed; the daughter, my Manda, a reduction photocopy.

Diamonds: I gave her no ring, she never let me forget.

my own boss: the competition's gaining, the yOGa academy's not done as well as she hoped.

Managing without men: her current guy just walked out.

saw a copy: she's been following my dismal career at a safe distance.

hates school: the kid's giving her a hard time.

meaning I don't know what: meaning precisely she'd like to put her on a plane and send her to guess who.

your mouth: my appetite

your other appetites: my other appetites

the camellia: I still love you.

My feelings exactly, or why did I write?

So one thing leads to another and suddenly I'm writing paper letters again, posted at the GPO, whose pigeons are mostly reliable.

Printed Letter

Dear Manda

Do pandas really eat ninety times their bodyweight of pretzels in one year? (Could you give up bamboo shoots for one year?) Are they really better than poppadums? Did you get the page 2 photos of Ash I sent by pigeon post? And the painting of the pomegranate in flower? Where are my EMINEM videos? When do you do La Scala? You're even more beautiful than Callas, but you

knew that. She had a worse nose but you have better hair. She
had a nicer noise but you have a better voise.

Hey, where's my pen? What's this printer doing in my study?
Whose computer is this?

Aha! Your Poppadum just woke up. Taco refrito, si.

But you know what the first thing I did with the new
computer was? I LEFT IT IN ITS BOX! Can you imagine? Can you
IMAGINE? The earthing was not right so the engineer who
came to install it just put his voltage meter back in his pocket and
walked out! And there it stayed in its box – four boxes actually:
computer, screen, printer and UPS battery – for the whole of May.
One MONTH! You would have DIED, my Manda!

So off I went to Mrs Goyal who runs a cybercafe down the
road and ran a Google search:
computer+earthing+safety+something+else and got an
Englishman in Korea who had the same problem and was getting
advice from everywhere. Look, an electrician said from Spain, just
wire the machine to the water pipes.

So I'm wired to the roof tank pipes! Shocking!

Then I went to the post office and bought 100 hours of Net
time, but couldn't make head nor tail of the Net server's dial-up
instructions. So ten hours later called in a young surdy engineer
who fixed it in ten seconds flat. There was a p missing in front of
the number. So I paid up 150/- for ten seconds.

Not even a capital P!

OK here's a quick lesson in computers:
0000000000000000000000000000000000000000000000000
1111111111111111111111111111111111111111111111111111111111111111111111

The whole thing, the surdy says, is based on combinations of
these two. You knew that? I know. But did you know the future's

HERE, not where you are? What's happening to this town? DVDs on every tree. Streets paved with pizza.

Look after mummy and bring her back. INVU.

Popp

Handwritten Letter, same envelope:

O,

It's been a wet monsoon. White ants ate the bamboo screen that was left rolled up on the floor of your room so I took it for a ride on the car roof rack. Now mould on your Chihuahua rug, like a patch of snow. White ants got into your cupboard too so I painted the shelves yesterday (and my right arm up to the elbow) with black creosote but should have changed into painting clothes. The tiger-stripe T shirt now has leopard spots. Can I change mine?

Come back. I promise to do my duty . . . . . . hang on: the gate. . . . let the maid in . . . must be 9:30 . . . toast, huevos rancheros . . .

Later. Villain Dilavar Singh also showed up. Now the boot's on the other foot. Little does he know he jump started this book. How his mask has changed! Smiles with half his mouth now: as if nature in its wisdom saved him for a stroke.

Forty-seven moons since you left. And nine days. Am back to sleeping at dawn. The mullah's wakeup call is the last thing I hear, and early birdsong. Wake up four hours later, high sun, underslept. Nowadays all my dreams are electronic. I back the Fiat at lightning speed around microchip bends as dogfights break out between swooping razorblades. Suddenly I'm in a helicopter and long-distance operators are giving me complicated instructions on how to land the bird in jail. I must snatch a software engineer in a liquid-crystal halter so provocative the raised matter on my credit card begins to smoke. Now why should this be?

Simple. I have a new computer! And a printer-scanner-copier-espresso machine. Your Tenderlion just succumbed to technobyte, O. It all happened in one go and you missed it. Come and see for yourself. You won't recognize the old house. You won't recognize the old town. Traffic lights, cash machines, pizza, a cattle pound.

A new world. You know, all through my childhood nothing changed outside and suddenly there's nothing but change. I swear I feel grateful to be around to witness it. Streets where there were just potholes. Eating places just up the road that weren't there last month. Why bother cooking? Miss your caldos though.

Come see my cash card. Cordless with caller ID? Our Pizza Hut?

(OK, there are still pigs at the gate, but better-natured pigs than before, more civil. And still a forest up the road, with real live wild boar.)

Tried to sleep last night, gave up at 1:30 and switched the computer back on and logged onto the Net. Daytime in America, still yesterday. NASA was going somewhere, stocks were doing something. Here just crickets and a moon softly waxing. So I pull out JC's letter with an important address. The acid test.

I type in: www.hermitagemuseum.com

Wait   (wait, wait) I'm in! Type <u>matisse</u> in the search box, click on The Red Room and . . . JCSolomon! – it's happening!

1:52 AM. a pink house emerges, roof first, building downwards, Mandy's pink house on a green hill, then bit by bit   trees sky   wallpaper

1:54   blonde head, first just the yellow bun   eyebrow eye

1:55   *fruit tabletop white wine decanter*

1:56   *red wine*

1:57   *Done. 60 million pinhead colours.*

Slow, I know. You have broadband, fat cables, fat everything. But images should download slowly or you miss the wonder. Remember the buzz?

You smile. 'A Native Discovers Downloading', by Doré.

OK watch him test his printer with Arab Coffeehouse, *race to the kitchen to put on the coffee pot, race back to watch the pale blue-grey ground develop. It's true: no joy like the first download – already it palls – but it kept me up till the mullah.*

Climbed up to the roof to do your exercises, then goodnight red planet (back this close in another 79,000 years), goodnight yellow streetlight (almost as bright), bed.

(Come back. The bed's too wide.)

Up at nine and straight to church, this desk the altar, the flat screen my grail. The machine is God. I learn obedience from the autosave icon: it blinks on, I leave the text as is. Automatic writing.

Have grown you a blue garden, come see, every flower blue.

The camellia is now by the gate, the mulberry where it was, putting out new green flags, so green you could wish you were a silkworm. Delete that. Insert: I just bought a digital egg-timer. (I did.) A lamp that comes on when you clap? (No I didn't. You still can't get those here.)

We'll get a TV, promise. You can watch your president.

Note for M enclosed. Please let her have it. Will you? Does she ask about me? Have you cut her hair?

Yours

oooooooooiooooooooooooooooooooooooooooooooooooooo

Red

(give up? A figure among ciphers. Turn it inside out for you: I'm all the ciphers and you're the only one)

PS. Our young voyager Z is in Petersburg on some scamfest or other; will he paint the town red or will it end up claiming him? We still meet for coffee. Barista you must see; it could be something next door to you in SOHO, but it's here!

Remember those Missing Person classifieds? Putli beti, Come home, all forgiven, no questions, Papa serious.

That's me.

N

C yberspace

All right, the Goyals have been around longer than I pretend. But it's all pretty new, even for the young folk bunched around the gate of every cyberacademy in this old new town. Matisse flattened space a hundred years ago, but we're just catching up. He'd have rejoiced to watch my slow downloads from St Petersburg, the Matisses especially.

My old laptop had megabytes; this machine has 80 *giga*bytes. *Eighty!* My books would rattle around in 1GB. What do I do with 79? I've found the free space every gipsy goes looking for when he closes his eyes at night. It was always out there among the stars. What will I do when wireless comes along? But no, by then I'm out of it: the clot that's biding its time knows.

This town is warping space too, the work of science, enterprise, and blind chance. A master plan is bashing streets through slums and suburbs, turning sleeping townsmen into a dazed citizenry. Coming down the road are the earthmovers, machines that only a few years ago belonged in pictures of far-off countries. Here are six men clinging to the cab of a big excavator. The driver's a wrangler: he bites so deep his wheels leave the ground; the other five are ballast, or maybe they just want to be there, touching their hero. No excitement like the new: unheard-of materials, monster machines, matter transformed. I felt it this afternoon walking by what just last year was a dismal hollow reserved for burnt-out leprosy cases. Drainage where there was none, houses where huts stood last month, shops that were shacks last week, stalls that were a midden. Patience and quiet pleasure in those whose lives were being transformed by a road, a pipe, a bridge. This is, I suppose, development; until now I never saw it happen.

Raised on the myth of underdevelopment, I exult: we're making something here, you bastards! But then the music from the temple loudspeaker sounds borrowed and I think: harmony has entered plainchant! Daily that space invades this. Are we moving to a grand synthesis or are we just starting to sound like them? Shouldn't we chuck all that? There are two aspects to this.

1. they built Rome, good for them (we have our work cut out)
2. they get the cream (keep some back)

Besides, this is richer, here. Wretchedness hasn't gone away (look behind that row of new shops) but it is no longer the rule, not in this city. People slip between the cracks (I watch my step) but we're getting there. We don't understand sanitation, even simple levelling, we've mislaid honesty, so the aesthetic sense was bound to atrophy, but perhaps the straight line will work its two-edged miracle. I used to fret that I would never live to see this country developed; now I'd rather watch the transformation. People have actually begun to *walk* differently.

I write differently too. For the first time I have a manuscript with no hard copy.

But, all right. I came late to the future. Here's how.

C offee

Zach has been milking the Net for all his thirties, and he must be thirty-five, give or take an hour. No grey, no thinning, just a tremor at the temples. The grey's in his clothes: slate jeans, taupe cotton T-shirt whose soft touch did for a woman's hand before I showed him the way. It took some pushing to get him on the Net too. Here we are at Barista, the only decent cafe in this one-horse *n-pig* town. Its walls acid-yellow showing through a sponged-on mottle overlay of orange, bold for the time, five years back. I'm wearing the collarless linen shirt Olivia loathed, lime-green braces and a paisley print lavender waistcoat. His T-shirt says INQUISITOR in front and HERETIC on the back. A couple of sitabout Anglos.

Z: *Used red saddlesex.*

N: What?

Z: Those were my waking dreamwords this morning. Crazy, eh? What the fornication could have brought that into the world? *Used red saddlesex.*

N: There are more things in heaven and earth, young Zachariah. Get on the Net and you'll see how small your town is.

Z: I thought the globe was meant to be shrinking.

N: It is, it's coming halfway to meet you. How do you think

those lovely Uzbekistani dancers got here last night? Uzbek Air? No, they got here on the Net. The Net brought them here, boy.

Z: There were lovely Uzbek dancers here last night?

N: The loveliest.

Z: You went and you didn't tell me?

N: You never answer your phone. You need to get out more, young Z. Get on the Web, get yourself a site. To market, to market, old sobersides! A is for @.

[*Draws an @ in the film of moisture that clings to the cold coffee glass and turns the glass around to face Z.*]

Z: They spend months organizing these festivals and then they forget to advertise.

N: You see? Same with you. And while you're about it get yourself a decent name. Add some desi Ks, some Vs or you'll get nowhere. India's the flavour, old son. *Zaccheus* just makes you invisible, one of them. They don't want them, they want us, for now. Go Sanskritize.

Z: And *you*?

N: I'm history. But you – you're too young to hide your talent under a bushel.

Z: Bushel of what?

N: [*Frowns, taking the question seriously.*] Coffee beans? Don't sidetrack. Listen to me. Get yourself a site, network like mad. Get off that high horse. Go West. I mean you don't actually have to go and *live* in New York and become a *paid*-up cocksucker. You can go trawl there now, for free! If what I read is true. One click and you're there. One click and you're back, thank God. Kiss the ground, this shitty ground, but get online, boy. Only black-shorts work in the dark. And God. And look at the mess He made.

[*Nods at the world outside the plate-glass window. An urchin gaping there.*]

Z: [*Follows N's gaze through the plate glass.*] Actually this is the rough sketch, the lit-up one. The fair copy He keeps hidden in a parallel slot in total darkness. Imagine a whole earth, complete in every detail down to you and me and this glass – minus the light. Think of the riches of sound laid bare!

Wednesday yabber, caffeine talking, but that night he goes and surfs the Net. And like magic, like that last match the little chimney-sweep lights in the story, he finds a contemporary-music festival in Adelaide. And he's off on his travels. No Ks no Vs. Zaccheus Wilding, Composer. He always reckons there's a *u* missing, and pretends it's spelt compos*eu*r, but I don't see him looking back.

Luck counts too, timing. With musicwallahs everything is tempo. This Petersburg 300th-anniversary bash came up just as he finished *Ashwamedha*. If he weren't kin once removed I'd be jealous.

All right, he found a niche, like any paanwallah. But it's a niche of one or two. You think writers are thin on the ground? Try writing *composer* on any form with a straight face in any country, never mind this one. Noise artist, if that. And yet – a nation mad for noise, dripping with it, shaking it off like a wet dog. It helps to have one bad ear, here. And a strong chin. Zach has both, and a long nose and a short tongue; listens hard, speaks when he must.

It took getting him connected to get me connected. Dilavar Singh pushed, Zach pulled. Now he knows I'm online I'll have a string of gloating messages in my inbox laughing at my surrender. But it worked for him. He'll come back dropping sly hints of conquest; let's see if he's got what it takes. Here he is in Petersburg with his newfound aunty.

Composeur

Zach wakes up in a reclining chair, his eyes filled with blinding light. It's not his room at the Petersburg Hilton. He's in the red studio facing the bright window beyond the hanging table. He is surrounded by paintings and picture frames and sculptures but the heart of the room is empty. The table is bare, where something happened last night. A voice he knows is calling and calling from somewhere: Breakfast! *Break*fast!

He looks around, plucks the white outlines of things. They twang like catgut and return to red silence.

She comes upstairs to get him.

'No room service here, sir.'

The Midwest *r* takes him back, again.

'Don't you have to be somewhere today?'

He shakes the red out of his eyes before he answers. Black would be kinder right now.

'Today?' Memory returns, the random access denied him earlier. 'Today's the Thai composer Boonsanong Somebody. I don't have to be there. He's one of the big wheels in Contemporary. *Silence with tub thumping* makes a statement about cultural invasion that every patriotic Russian will want to hear. I'm told he hands out earplugs at the entrance, but don't let me put you off.'

'I can't wait!' She pulls him up into a kiss. 'And tomorrow?'

'Tomorrow is someone else and the next day is me – but you're not to come.'

'That's not fair.'

'No, really. Promise me you won't. I don't like what they've done to it. Cuts, stand-ins, make-do. They're only playing it because it's half an hour shorter than the competition.'

'Which is what?'

'The Algerian entry. *Batutisme*. The guy's an exile, lives in France.'

'What's it about, yours?'

'It's called *Ashwamedha*, which means horse sacrifice.'

'Horse sacrifice?'

'It was a sovereignty ritual kings used in ancient times. They let a special horse roam free with their markings and anybody who refused to let it pass was considered a rebel. It was a way of demarcating your kingdom. If you were a good vassal you honoured the horse and let it go. Or you got clobbered. In the end the horse was sacrificed, but first the queen had to lie with it.'

She rolls her eyes, and lets them widen to accommodate the picture that zinged in there. 'They had a queen like that here. Catherine the Great. Only she was the one that died.'

'Yeah, maybe that bit caught the selectors' eye. They've done one rehearsal, but it doesn't sound like I heard it in my head. I mean, I'm not complaining. You're lucky to hear anything you write, ever, although there's a melody in it you actually do hear in the street. From wandering minstrels selling one-string violins.'

'*Ektara*,' she offers. The pronunciation is foreign but he's amazed. Her smile says: 'I may not have spent four years in your country but I know a thing or two.'

He shakes his head, impressed; it's not like she said *sitar* or *Ravi Shankar*. He's scored the piece for ektara and harvest drum but they've substituted a tabla. And if their tabla master can't read notation it makes perfect sense for him to play what he knows and smile at the score as if it were a stranger on a bus.

'Is it all Indian instruments?'

'Oh no. I've snuck in bassoon to cover for shehnai in the darker passages. At the end there should be a giant Japanese drum and gong, but you can't have everything.'

In the bathroom there's a little Air France toiletries set she got from the aeroplane. He thinks as he brushes his teeth: are women more likely to carry off aeroplane stuff? All the little punnets of honey and cheese and cologne. Men take the headphones. A T-shirt on a hook reads AVERAGE WHITE TRASH on one side; he means to check the other (back or front?) but is distracted by the garment on the next hook.

It's the red-lace panties. From the day before. Mostly cord as far as he can see, elastic cord and mesh and gauze and lace and nothing.

But *are* they the same? Was he mistaken about the line of red lace? Can you be sure of the colour of a *line*?

'There *is* an appointment I'm missing today,' he confesses over breakfast, 'but at home, not here. Two appointments, actually: Wednesday morning coffee with a friend in the only cafe in town. And something cultural – *folkloric* as they say here – starting today. A ten-day festival that comes every three years. The festival I can miss but the coffee is obligatory. And me a tea man.'

'Why didn't you tell me? What does she do?'

'He. He's a writer, quite well known. N – – –.'

She shakes her head.

'I mean at home, he has a following. Anyway I'm pretty sure I'm in his next book. What *he* doesn't realize is I'm taping him too.'

[*Villain! I should have known.*]

'What, like under the table?' she laughs.

The red table hangs between them for a moment then is gone. Her body a white ghost spreadeagled there.

'Ya,' – he leans over and kisses her lightly on each knee – 'it's too far gone to come clean. Anyway, it's for posterity, it's for him. But also I need a highfalutin voice-over for something I'm doing.'

'What's the cafe *like*?' She can't imagine.

'Barista? Straightforward turn-of-the-century. This century.'

'Just trying to picture it.'

'Come and see. No – don't.'

'Why not?' But she knows, can guess.

'It's shitty, the streets. Sometimes you could scream.'

She guessed. Prickly third-worlder. 'So there you are filing reports on each other. Like good Russian citizens in the bad old days.'

'Yeah. Only not with the state – with our computers.'

[*Varlet! To think I wrote the libretto for his operetta The Manes of Mrs Mani. Set in the 22nd century, I recall a line that went: 'The State didn't wither away – it flowered into the Universal Hard Disk.'*]

'Still sounds a bit shifty.'

[*Decidedly, methinks.*]

'When the universal hard disk crashes and barbarism returns, my perfidiousness will stand justified. [*The knave doth steal my lines for witty table talk and pretend it's for my good!*] Can you see the tablet? HE PRESERVED CIVILIZATION IN THIS OUTPOST WHEN IT KNEW NOT IT WAS DOOMED.'

'And you?'

'I just rearranged the sounds.'

'Composer, eh? Eat up, we're going for a run.'

D *is for* D onut

See also D ariya Dun, D om, *etc*

D ariya Dun

Our city is barely four hundred years old. The dun (*see*) in which it sits is the last of the wrinkles formed by the collision of Gondwanaland with the Asiatic landmass, the first being the snowy crest of the highest Himalayas. An early apeman evolved here. In the long pre-Hindu dawn it was occupied by indigenes whose descendants live on in modern bondage in the valley; in Vedic times elaborate sacrifices including the horse sacrifice were performed here. Buddhist missionaries would have passed through; then Muslims arrived, a Sikh janissary planted a flag. Neighbouring Nepali kings laid claim to the valley, the British annexed it, and now it is the capital of a hill state in the union of India. For hundreds, thousands of years, the valley slept, not always peacefully, but in the past two or three years it has woken up.

Two or three years! Imagine what it means to be able to say that. Whole lifetimes were spent in unchanging villages or towns once. And here is change on an unimaginable scale in a matter of years, even months. Of course you'll say people have felt this way before. When the railway arrived here a hundred years ago they said: the dawn of a new age! But after the first terrible clanking and hooting of engines, the city fell asleep.

It will not sleep again. My new computer is part of this waking into sleeplessness. I'm like the villager who leaves off wearing a dhoti and takes to pants. It's a private decision with public consequences. Others see, follow, and larger changes come to stay. A canal I loved as a boy, a torrent of chill mountain water that fell by roaring stages, has been covered over. I carried the last scattered stone blocks home one by one and made a memorial garden seat. The lifting may have hurt my heart, but the wound went deeper. Last summer I saw a stack of kerbstones on the road that replaced it and stopped to stare. *Kerb*stones, here! A frontier had been crossed.

Nowhere else I know has the change gone so deep. Last year I saw wholesale change in China, old Canton transformed. This is piecemeal, less magical, more telling. New and old argue the point, but the new has already won. And the change is unrelenting. Delhi asked for it, others wished for it; we had it thrust upon us. When a new hill state was formed we went overnight from retirement town to capital city.

Once upon a time the city, any city, meant light; now it means noise. *Sound*, young Z would say, not noise. But *Send peace in our time, O Lord* is a good prayer. At night ambulances howl, a new noise; there were none just a few years ago. You rented a taxi or a rickshaw; a few years ago I saw a concussion patient trundled through the streets on a trolley with castors. Today white vans prowl looking for custom, the word AMBULANCE painted backwards importantly under the windscreen, a proud theft from foreign TV. The jackals of my earliest childhood, whose yowling first set a horizon, have disappeared. Think of it: a presence older than Aesop vanished just the other day.

Still, the streets are better lit, and better paved. Traffic lights work, are mostly obeyed. Water pressure in the mains is up (in the right suburbs), garbage is collected (then dumped short of the bin). Plate-glass shopfronts, neon signs, chrome, cash machines; this afternoon I saw a red umbrella advertising coffee. An organic-food outlet opened last month, multiplex cinemas are promised, where there will certainly be buttered popcorn. A metropolitan girl has appeared in the half-made streets, rare but there. There's one who walks her dog past our gate (I *want* it to piss on the privet) who could be an Italian film star. I look out through the gate and see jeans on a peon, a T-shirt on a tramp, shorts on the retired Mr Singh. Olivia could take her Junoesque form jogging and nobody, well not everybody, would look. Manda would fit in but would she stay?

So we step out of the old frame. The other day I saw a mitre box at a picture framer's, home-made, approximate, but there. On every side the right angle encroaches on chaos; ruled edges replace the old smudge. One thing we still lack: a public library. This is like not having a library in Boston. I want to shout: Libraries of the World, send us your discards! The Doon Library Project, Old Jail, Dehra Dun, UA 248001 India. They can even be in serif. [Last proof change, Sam – cut off my hands!]

Here, halfway around the world from Z and A, the day's just begun. Sun still under the hill, all the neighbourhood TVs spouting religion, mustard oil pouring yellow into begging bowls with black tin cutouts of Kali. Saturday. Saturn's frownday, dread day of Jove, giving unto beggars day. Placating day, watch-your-step day, chanting pouring like oil from temple loudspeakers.

The sun comes up, gilds old lady Grewal's veil as she goes about her ambulant prayer. Up and down the garden she goes, her prayer line returning to *A4 A4 A4*. It always sounds like *A4*: she's praying for snow-white bond. The city wakes.

Bedtime, for me.

D om

The aborigines of India, treated as slaves by all later invaders
except the British. Outcastes for the last three millennia, settled
on the worst land, they live by menial work, the most odious
tasks such as the handling of excreta and corpses being reserved
for them. The more independent among them prefer an itinerant
life as jobbers such as blacksmiths and tailors, or entertainers
such as bear-tamers and acrobats. Reviled for their filth, they are
denied water where they might wash; in villages they may not
use the same well or spring as their betters. In former times it
was an offence for one to let his shadow fall on a person of high
caste; in some parts merely being seen was to cause pollution.
Sumptuary laws forbade the wearing of any garment below the
knee, the punishment decapitation. When a group split off and
travelled west eventually forming the gipsies of Europe, their
chosen word for themselves was Rom, a variant of Dom.

Their worship was animistic, a propitiation of malign nature
that frequently included snake worship. The cobra, or nag, was
especially venerated; this and other elements of their ancient
faith was absorbed into the iconography of new religions such as
Hinduism. Nagsidh, a wooded spur to the south of our city, would

have been one of their sacred sites; today a Shiva temple stands there. Christian missionaries while improving the lot of the Dom repeated the old folly of presuming to supplant their faith. Over the centuries the Doms have drifted in and out of Hinduism, Buddhism, Islam and Christianity but seldom cared for even the nominal observances of their choice of the moment, preferring the demons and fairies of local tradition ancient and modern.

The existence of a large section of doubtful brahmins and rajputs in these hills suggests a gradual sanskritization of earlier arrivals, but the Doms either remained subjugated or themselves resisted acculturation. The constitution forbids discrimination on the basis of caste; subsequent legislation has attempted positive discrimination to redress old wrongs. New names and jobs bring relief to some; others refuse a subtler slavery and find release in drink, dreaming perhaps of a lost age when gods were more dangerous than men.

D onut fried cake with nothing in the middle

I have just destroyed five floppy disks. Taken them apart like clams, cracked their shells, pulled out the surprising slippery tongues. (What did I expect to find?) They were defunct but I felt like a thief all the same, breaking and entering. At last the word disk makes sense, the square is circled. They're disks all right, and floppy, with an empty centre. A two-dimensional donut. When I have parted each one from its little clanking locomotive wheel, the heap looks antiquated, industrial. Twentieth century. A pen-and-ink man, I was always uncomfortable with floppies, but I learnt to live with them without ever looking inside. Now I must learn to live with another donut, the compact disc, which still shines like the future, though I can't credit all the binaries packed into a single pit in its surface. No question of an inside; there is only surface.

The other day I saw a scientist's mock-up of the universe. It too resembled a sugar donut. Am I just hungry?

D aughter a creature who will not stay

D eath (proof of life after) *see* D ullsville

D elhi a good lover but a bad wife

D ownloading

Here is a trick. While waiting for a painting to download take two spoons of coffee and percolate directly into a cup. Now take two sheets of card and lay them on the picture; vary the gap and the angles as you please for astonishing random views the painter never intended (or had himself) always noting marriages he did intend: colour with colour. Be humbled, be exalted.

Alternatively: wrap a comb in tissue paper and blow gently.

D ullsville *see* D ariya Dun

Dun a valley, but also a rise, in the way *down* can mean an upland

E *is for* E nter

See also E kalavya, E asement

E nter *as in* to break and enter

The riverbed is wide and dry and covered in smooth white stones that catch the late rising last quarter-moon. A black rope of water unravels at this heap of boulders that the men use to cross to the other bank. The house they want sits on a knoll overlooking the valley. The gate is on the main road at the head of a long drive; this approach is straight up the riverbank to the back wall. The owners are away, Paltaniya has learnt through his network of jobbing whitewashers. It's a steep climb, slow but not impossible if you use as hand- and footholds the young eucalypts that always seem to find the perpendicular.

From tree to tree the men climb, shadows handing down a cargo of silver trunks.

The houseowners are city folk, artists with one foot in the countryside. The gate plaque reads *Meghaduta* in an ancient script so stylized as to be barely recognizable. The lady has been meaning to redo it in ceramic in plain Roman; till then it's brass. The blackshorts, who – except for Gilgitan – can't read, come up from the opposite end of the property. No dogs, they've learnt, no need for poisoned meat.

His Snakeship is first to the front door, handling the padlock.

Brass, 7 levers, Harrison. Standard. Then some kind of built-in lock that a child could push past. Still, a side door might be simpler. They do a circuit of the house following the winding veranda. Potted ferns and bleached driftwood antlers reach out for their bare feet. A Victorian hatstand leans at the back door with an antique sola topi on a hook. Gilgitan tries on the hat and leaves it on his head. His Snakeship goes to say something and lets it go. They return to the front veranda as Phuljari appears from the garden with a pickaxe in one hand and an axleshaft smith-beaten to an edge at one end. People, his smile says, will leave gardening aids around for blackshorts.

They bend the bolt with some minor splintering of wood. The door opens. Nagouri is with them or this would be too easy. His Snakeship leads the way in, left foot first. They are in total darkness. Always this is the tense moment and every man, every time, is tempted to flatten himself against a wall to escape the gunshot. Gilgitan tilts his head in his saurian way to look up and down and sideways from under the rim of the hat. It's so dark he can't even see old Phuljari standing right next to him.

'*NAMASTE*,' comes a voice from straight ahead at the other end of the room.

The men jump or freeze, according to their nature.

'Welcome,' the voice continues, enunciating for effect, 'come on in.' This is radio Hindi.

The men step back, still facing forwards, in a kind of blind ballet of retreat.

Light floods the room.

The men turn and make a run for it, first the untidy small-stepped scramble of a herd, then they're out in the open and flying across the lawn, leaping the low stone boundary. It's there, in the ditch on the other side, they discover no one's giving chase.

Gilgitan has lagged behind. He's standing hatted on the lawn, one hand under his chin, one hand beckoning them. Standing under the sky, looking back at the house through the open front door. There's no one there, he's sure, and he doesn't believe in ghosts, mostly.

'It'll be a recording,' he whispers all the same when they come up. He's heard of such things rigged to scare off intruders.

His Snakeship, who was first through the door, stays where he is on the lawn. Gilgitan makes to go back in alone; he trusts his instinct in these matters. When Chhanga and Vinod offer to follow, His Snakeship sends Phuljari to scout around the house once more and waits till he returns. Cocky youths don't impress him. Phuljari returns from his tour satisfied. They go back in together, older cautious heads.

They are in a large sparsely furnished sitting room whose walls are hung with paintings from end to end. His Snakeship crosses to a door in the far wall without glancing at the curios on the end tables; drawing rooms seldom have valuables of the kind he's after. Jewellery, gold, silver, pocketable stuff, live in bedrooms. Vases and TVs and gilt frames can go hang.

Gilgitan has tilted the pith helmet right back and is stepping along the walls examining the pictures. He has never seen a naked woman framed on a wall. Or a cross-legged saint with the sky and the sun and the moon in the space where his chest should be. This he likes. One with antelope leaping over a trafficked city road while the zebras wait patiently at their crossing. And this one, just a saffron swirl with needles of gold in it. Gilgitan steps back to frown at the abstraction with his head on one side.

'Piss all,' mutters His Snakeship, coming back into the room. Again he's inclined to tick Gilgitan off for wasting time, but doesn't.

'Here,' Vinod calls from another bedroom.

They troop in there, Gilgitan with a backward glance at the paintings. But the drawer that Vinod has emptied on the bed has jade beads and baubles, costume jewellery. Drawer by drawer they empty the chest, growing rougher with every disappointment, scattering the contents, kicking through them, chucking, ripping, tossing.

Nothing. Not a fart in a bottle.

'Look at this,' Phuljari calls from the drawing room. He's found the tape recorder. He lifts the machine with both hands and draws it back towards himself as if to say *mine*, as the men gather around.

'Play it back again,' Gilgitan says and presses the rewind button.

Vinod is impressed. He wouldn't know which button to press, but His Snakeship's patience has worn thin. He yanks the plug out at the wall and crosses to an alcove they missed by the front door where there's a desk with many pigeon holes. Chequebooks, calling cards, a glue stick, postage stamps rain onto the floor as his probing finger flicks. Envelopes, folders, brochures, maps. On the top shelf are books – hold on, something blue and gold falls onto the baize. It's a passport. That's worth money. Slipped among the paperbacks, the slim volumes of poetry, the owners have secreted their second passports. Any more? His Snakeship lifts a random cut of books. Something sticking out of the top is not a bookmark; it's a five-hundred-rupee note!

The men ransack the bookcase. Book by book, page by page;

never have they studied books so closely. They stand there in their black shorts and greased bodies leafing gravely through the volumes: magi at the solstice undress ball. In the end they're holding the books by the spines and fanning them downwards. Notes cascade down, clean new notes, so unlike the soiled notes they've always handled that they're inclined to doubt their authenticity. Gilgitan holds one up against the light. It's real all right, he pronounces as Gandhi's head smiles back at him from the ghostly watermark. They shake down every book. Money, money, money. Phuljari grins vacantly, Chhanga is awestruck; they have never seen such a shower. When it stops raining Vinod gathers it all up, their treasurer, shuffles and pats and tidies the notes into a single crisp bundle and hands it over to His Snakeship.

Gilgitan has already wandered back into the drawing room. There's a painting he must see again. He stands in front of it and is immediately sucked into its space. There's a woman in there at the window of her bedchamber looking out at the sky where the remnant of a storm broods. Dawn has painted the east pink but a sad blue light bathes the forecourt of the house where the front door stands open and an old watchman sleeps. Someone has slipped out at the door and vanished – or did he see a movement in the cypress tree beside the window?

'Let's go,' Nag hisses. They've done well, thanks to one sticking-out note.

Gilgitan strains away from the painting but anyone can see the cord of his gaze is unbroken even when his eyes settle unseeingly on His Snakeship.

'What?'

'Let's get out of here,' Nag repeats, his snake eye flashing. He's accustomed to obedience, but of all the gang this lizard is the hardest to hypnotize.

'Come on, Gilgitan!' old Phuljari urges; his voice has the padded rubberstamp fall of a deputy who still thinks he'll be leader. Leave together, break up on the way home, is the rule.

Gilgitan shoulders off the voices. He has taken the painting down from the wall and holds it in both hands. Here is a second transgression: things that can be palmed or otherwise secreted on the person are all the booty tradition allows. Humming to himself he holds the picture up to catch the bright light, the one that scared them. But the branch that shook by the window where the woman sighs is still again and silent. Gilgitan strains through the glass.

His mates are not there, the frame is not there, there's just him and this woman. He wants this woman. She reminds him of the pig girl; he thinks of her pout last night as she whispered: *You weren't supposed to come inside, Gillu.* Often he's thought this before, with the pig girl, with the truck paintings. Entering a painting is like entering a woman. No moment like that, not even the spending.

It's the first time, of all these times when he's entered houses full of things, things that sit there so still and rooted you'd think there was a string that attached them, every single one, to their rightful owners, those slick geckos you see in the streets spinning their car keys on one finger, the first time he's been tempted to take something he can't exchange or flog off the next day. Something to keep, to own.

He will have her. Termites have bored, with the unerring precision of an immense and infinite not to say godly randomness, through her two eyes: she looks like she's hoarding light; he

wants that bright thing, to keep, to measure, to paint. He drops
where he stands, so suddenly his knees could be greased, and
squatting on his hams he lifts the frame and raps hard on the
floor with one corner so the glass cracks and the mitred slats leap
apart. Bared waists of three fine nails stand in his way. Glass
pieces fan open like fingers as he pulls the slats apart and as he
reaches into the gap to free the lady blood spurts from his thumb,
fuckwit Gillu, and a droplet falls on the woman's neck, another
ruby, so he changes hands and coaxes the painting out of its jail,
rocking the paper gently as he pulls. She slides out into his hands,
free for the first time in years, breathing air, night air straight
into her small convex nose, but he wants no more blood on her
so he looks wildly around for a cloth and jumps up, finds the
corner of a cloth on the nearest sideboard and tugs so sharply
the bowl of rose petals simply jumps and stays where it is. He
scrolls the painting in it, tucks it into his waistband and lopes out
of the house and across the grass, grinning in the dark. Just
taking back, giving back, a little free space.

It's only at the bottom of the hill as the throbbing begins in
his hand that he remembers a neglected duty. He was supposed
to leave a calling card of the Black Codpiece Society at the door.
Instead he squats down now by the river and leaves it here, a
good firm turd, then washes with his good hand and reties his
langot so the princess nestles in there in high hard company.
Then runs, skipping, hopping, leaping, hooting in a straight line
towards chilli pork and rice and hemp-weed fritters.

E kalavya

Ekalavya was an outcaste archer in the valley of the Doon. One day he went to Drona and said: Great Guru, no one is a greater master of archery than you. Teach me. Black dog of a Dom! Drona replied. Eyes down! You dare to come to me when your very glance defiles! Never will you master archery. But Ekalavya returned to the forest and fashioned a clay image of Drona and bowing down before it took instruction from the absent master. So accomplished did he grow that he could shoot a fruit bat in the eye on the darkest night in the farthest tree if it so much as blinked. One day the warrior Arjun, who aspired to be first among caste marksmen, went to his master Drona and said: You promised to make me the best yet word has it there is an archer in the forest who can shoot seven arrows into the mouth of a red dog if it bark but once. Impossible, said Drona, and together they went into the forest to lay the false rumour. But there they found Ekalavya shooting hyenas by the mere echo of their laughter. What is this, cur? demanded Drona. An effigy of you, great master, said Ekalavya, bowing low. All I have learnt I owe you. Then where is my price, wretch? You have only to ask, your honour, replied Eklavya without lifting his eyes. Give me, then, said Drona, that same thumb that holds the arrow steady in the string. Gladly, your worship, said Ekalavya, and straightway cut off his right thumb. And that is how Arjun the wheat-skinned came to be the greatest archer in Hindoostan.

E. V. Widdershin, *History of the Peoples of Hindoostan*, Leipzig: Einthof Verlag, 1837.

The story is set in this valley but it happened everywhere, throughout the country where settler met hunter and tricked him out of his land and his faith. Ekalavya's descendants scavenge among rubbish heaps and clean out your septic tank. When they can they steal. There are colleges named after Drona; I have yet to see an Ekalavya Public School.

Some day there will be a severed thumb in bronze up on a pedestal, but it will drip blood and sweat, as long as there are Dronacharyas.

E asement right of way across another's land

Some twenty years ago, after renting all their lives, my parents decided to build in this valley. In the old days Anglos always rented; home was somewhere else. So we were pioneers of a sort. The land we bought needed clearing; most plots on this former racecourse, once the most picturesque in the country, were overgrown. Even after the builders left there was a thicket of lantana and marijuana behind the house that only gradually gave way to a garden. One day the washerman's son playing in the yard gave a shout and sprang back from his game as a king cobra, whose bite kills quickly, flashed past him along the boundary wall. It never returned. At one time more people died of snakebite than of heart attacks. Today even the frogs are disappearing.

Ten years ago I enclosed a piece of land beyond our front boundary wall, public land, and planted flowering trees there. Later the municipality and the forest department sanctioned the encroachment by encouraging every homeowner to enclose and plant a plot. The trees have grown – Brazilian coral bean (scarlet), Mexican silk cotton (pink and yellow), Chinese golden shower (dread dominatrix), even a neem, rare in this wet valley – and now we have a green belt between us and the road. And a third yard, with a private gate. The ragpickers – Doms to a man but usually women and children – have lost an equal share of forage territory; here is the whole history of enclosures writ small. But the pigs and stray dogs don't get to foul up the frontage and the denuded valley has some twenty new trees. A man came yesterday to collect the loppings for firewood, people waiting for a passing tempo use the shade of the camel hoof (or purple Bauhinia) at the corner. Sometimes people stop simply to admire the seasonal blossom on the trees. Last summer we lost one of a pair of mimusops, slow-growing hardwoods with a scented white flower, to a freak windstorm; a willow stake is thriving where it stood. Golden privet rings the enclosure; the gold of the hedge is public property.

In the last rains I improvised a hinged valve over our storm-water sluice to stop flooding of the front lawn from the drain beyond the wall. It was aluminium, grouted into the wall on the outside and worked perfectly. It lasted one monsoon. The problem was not mechanical. The vane was simply too shiny. Four square inches of aluminium was worth stealing. I still see the woman go by who very likely took it; she is forty, could have grown-up children (say, a pig girl of twenty), has not bathed for weeks, has worn the same sari for years and carries an empty cement sack on her shoulder. Her eyes are on the ground as she steps around the privet hedge looking for anything that glitters, or possibly just an easement.

F *is for* F ace

See also F amily

F ace 1

On the third day, Saturday, Zach goes back again to the Matisse room. He's still aching from yesterday's run and Aline wants to take him to Pushkin, to walk in the park and show him the red squirrels, so he pleads an appointment and goes instead back to the Hermitage. He has one week in Petersburg and there is nothing he particularly wants to see by way of the sights. He needs to see the Matisse room again because he feels the stirrings of a notion, a rhombus of four notes he'd like to tease out in his head in front of the painting. At the moment it sounds in his bad ear like the blather of the big drum that ends *Ashwamedha*.

It's work, no lie, but he goes also because he must put some distance between himself and this woman who has suddenly entered his life. She had the courage, or is it skill, to pick him up and he didn't have what it takes to refuse. He needs space to think, space to – what? Space, simply.

And he needs to see if she is there, that other one in black, whose face torments him because he didn't see it.

It's a fine fall day. Petersburg shines pale blue and yellow outside the south-facing windows of the Hermitage. From the third floor the whole paved expanse of Dvortsovaya Square flips up in the sunshine silver grey and grained like fishscales or a flat screen waiting for a painting to download. Matisse wouldn't automatically be out there.

'No plein aire for him,' Zach remembers Aline saying as they came out into the open. 'He was a studio painter.'

He turns away from the window and passes through the Picasso room, his eye already seeking out the end of the bench, her bench, as he approaches the doorway into the next room.

She's there!

Sitting exactly as before, in black, her head a blaze of red.

He stops in his tracks. He wanted to see her, never for a moment imagining he would, and now she's there he's afraid. There's a tension in the line of her that says DANGER 10,000 VOLTS. He feels the preternatural charge in his fingers as if the very air that prowls about her had suddenly turned to face the threat it sensed in his approach – while she remains unmoving. There's a weirdness almost audible in the assisted daylight, as if her red and black have conspired to make a witch of her. He wills himself forward, finds he can walk, comes up behind.

But there's no window in her back, no thin red line of lace.

Red hair bound in stooks, and the black dress which he now sees is a sort of lace mantilla over silk over a gauze blouse. The pair of pale moons sticking out of green stockings are her knees. The last time he was so absorbed in the back he caught no glimpse of her face; he hasn't the faintest idea what she looks like. As if reading his mind she turns with an owl-like twist of the head and looks at him. He holds the tight anxious searching look, finds the bead threaded with recognition: then she snaps the thread and goes.

Young, is his first thought, but, god, identical. The exact total with age subtracted from the sum. The same green eyes, same straight-on Russian ikon nose, riverstone chin, slice-of-watermelon mouth. Only a rogue gene could have paired this top and bottom lip, fine coupling with coarse on some riverbank thirty thousand years ago. Red eyebrows that climb steeply to dip at the very end; real eyelashes. Aline's face, only half her life ago.

She's tried to spite it, dumb it down, has stuck two studs, steel, one a spike, in the flesh of the left cheek, gone gothic pancake white (the pancake stops a deliberate inch short of ears and neck and hairline), crimsoned the hair, dibbled pipblack lipstick. But it's a face to paint, down all the ages.

Zach would follow, and follow, but the same forbidding aura that clothed her sitting wraps around her going. She pulls the mantilla about her and walks off, her arms folded tightly in front of her violet bustier, her black lips set. A black band about her throat like a ruff to hide a throat operation. He has the impression of indigo gauze over fuzzy white arms, and memory or desire supplies, after she's well gone, a fringed black suede skirt, green boots and ten yards of red bootlace.

He stands there rigid; then turns slowly back to the painting. *The Painter's Family.* The girl in it has not moved but there's a breathing colour in her cheek that wasn't there before. He's so sure he'd reach out and touch but there's a guard in the room. He stares at the picture. It's in turmoil, everything in it in suspension. The colours swarm, light dazzles, a pindrop on the rug is heard throughout the painting. Nothing is further away from anything else than anything else. It's some time before he realizes his focus is not on the surface of the painting but somewhere beyond, where the horizon might be. When he does he tries to keep his focus there but loses it to the plane of the canvas and can't get it back again. He was starting to see things in there, it was just starting to get interesting. Like a peeled-off glove, fingers half inside out, or an echo running ahead of the sound.

From childhood on, Zach has been tormented by a visual dimension to the music he hears: odd shapes appear on his retina at the moment of notation, a comb, say, its teeth elongating like ectoplasm. Sometimes he will sketch these ladders, these spiral stairs, and espaliered trees of sound, but he knows even as he scribbles they're simply graphic analogues emptied of the music that lent them meaning. If he could only move the other way, he thinks, move from holograms to sound. Painters make still music, why can't he paint by ear?

He feels an interloper in this painted room. The figures trapped in the painting have retreated into a depth beyond contact. He closes his eyes. Here in the living world people suddenly come up so close you can't see them, or for that matter yourself. The painter knows this, has felt it in his bones, and from that frustration has made of his family an emblem of dense but open space. He's spread the room out on a single plane so each individual exists almost in a bubble, a separate oxygen tent.

The music grinds to a halt and dies.

It's gone and Zach knows it's pointless waiting. But sits down where she sat. The seat is hot. He endures the burn, expecting that, then gets up and leaves the building.

Not chasing today, but tracking.

'You have a daughter.'

He's back at the griffin mews. She's waited in for him.

'You don't have a cellphone?' She asks a prior question now.

'No.'

'Yes.'

'And her father?'

'We're . . .' her eyes drop, count three dots, 'separated.'

'Is he Russian?'

'French.'

'In France?'

'Paris. Any more questions?'

'One more. What am I?'

She doesn't pretend confusion. 'You mean like, toy boy? No, the real thing. This doesn't happen all the time. Does it with you?'

'It happens.'

'Now and then?'

'More then than now.' That's nearer the truth. Dorian girls, and the one, a long way off campus, he left behind. Before returning to give himself to music, a starry desert of sound, every new work a shifting dune, notes piling up like grains of sand, burying the past.

'Kiss me, Zach. Just a little nothing kiss.'

He just stands there, so she drops onto the beanbag.

'So how do you do all that?' She waves at the room down the passage. 'Like your heart's in it.'

'Did I say it wasn't?'

He looks at the mouth he kissed last night and sees the mismatched lips on the daughter. The same slice of watermelon, a little bruised, crystallizing, one day along. This older, sweeter red could smother him. Smothering he can take, but mothering? Last year *Metronome* clubbed him, somehow, with composers under thirty. They acknowledged the error in the next issue, but he could pass. The daughter's a kid, she looks a proper bitch. And the mother is tender and trusting and real and so suddenly and completely yielding, it's – what? Scary? No, *unreal*. More unreal than the fantasy in the gallery just now. That worries him.

'All right. I should have known she was here. I'm an irresponsible mother, in the eyes of the law. Her father won't have anything to do with me. I'm a bad influence, apparently. Or it could be that I cut up his Picasso. Anyway, he got a court order, had her taken away. But she has a way of catching up: she can't stay with me and she can't stay away. I guess this time she got here ahead of me. She used to come in here and ransack this place until I got the code changed.'

'What's her name?'

'Red.'

'Sorry, stupid question.'

'Sorry we're dysfunctional.' She makes a mock bow where she sits. 'You want to see an average family? Here.'

She jumps up and switches on the plasma screen, calls up her pictures and clicks on one. 'Remember this?'

It's the painting he's just been standing in front of.

F amily

'First of all he's not in the picture, but that's OK. Lots of painters did that, including my father.'

'Your father?'

'Aaron Medlar. Ever hear of him?' It's always hard to get that out but she can say it easily to a foreigner. He's entitled not to know.

'The apple-pie man!'

'The same. You know *Family with Apple Pie*?'

'I had a poster of *Cochise with Apple Pie*.'

'It's in my pictures.' She waves the wireless mouse. 'And *Apple Pie at Wounded Knee*, and all the rest. He'd always squirm over the money that one made. Donated it and all, but I didn't hold it against him. I thought he was great. Till he started to like the money he made.'

'Serious money?'

Come on, her look says: when did painters make serious money? 'Jester money, small-time big, like entertainers make, movie stars. But he married again, after my mother died. You know the Holemeal chain?'

'Healthy donuts? I was an addict.'

'He married the daughter. Armenians – from Calcutta – she was not a lot older than me. One critic called it a merger. It was marking time really, she was terminal. With my mother it was different. They actually got along, no squabbling, no philandering, and no childhood scars for me. So not only do I get to live in his shadow, he goes and steals my pain. I guess Holemeal wasn't serious money either. So he found me a husband.'

'I didn't think you lot went in for that sort of thing.'

'Believe it. Now I think he'd be satisfied, if he were around.'

'And you went along?'

'What do you know at nineteen? What do you know at ninety? He was handsome, smart. Almost in the Fortune 50. *Still* almost – that really hurts.

'Anyway. Here's *this* painter's family. Matisse is forty-two, he's a success, he's making money, he has a good wife, a daughter, two sons, he should be happy. And he is, but sometimes he wonders if he was better off when he was free, a struggling painter with a mistress and nothing in the world but light. So he does this painting, a portrait of his life. *The Painter's Family*, minus the painter, but his life's on the line again.'

They're back in the living room at Issy, with Madame Matisse on the sofa absorbed in her needlework to one side and the boys Pierre and Jean in the centre playing their game of draughts. Their half-sister Marguerite dominates the right side of the painting, the only one looking out of the frame. With six red brushstrokes Matisse outlines her features and captures her youth and diffidence. The red of her hair is dulled by the cream of the wallpaper behind it but the painting is flooded with light, almost more southern light than the northern interior can sustain; it's as if Matisse has willed it bright.

RED

'Matisse is missing, that's his wife Amelie, in the same room as her children but she could be a million miles away; they're all in the same picture but they could be on different continents. The boys are separated by a chequerboard, it could be the earth, the daughter's on another planet. They're there and not there, but it's not a cold painting, is it? You don't feel like he's a long way off: I mean, you can almost see his foot, like you do in some of the sketches. He's close to them in his own way, but what he's really close to is his work. It's like they're in the way so he figures why not use them, put them in. I kind of always got that feeling with my own father. He was a good father, but it was like he didn't see me. Sometimes I'd want to wave in his face and say, I'm here, Pop.'

She waves up from the beanbag, a girl again; he sees the face in the face.

'So there they are, all pinned out, no resentment, maybe even love, but mainly detachment. Except Marguerite won't stay pinned. That's the daughter. The others are happy to be in the picture, well maybe happy's too strong a word, maybe they haven't noticed; Marguerite has: she wants out. And he kind of knows how she feels. He's given her this faraway look, and green clogs. Nice daddy.'

Zach is looking at the girl. She's like a black wedge driven into a bright painting. He's also got an eye on Aline as she sits there stroking the mouse. She's drifted off into the picture, into her own picture. She has an expression that almost matches the daughter's, this daughter in the picture and her own. Strange, he thinks, like a Martian; first they come right up to you, humans, then suddenly they go so far away you can't even see yourself truly, because they showed you what you are.

Right then she turns and catches his assessing gaze and smiles sadly.

'You had a daddy like that, Zachy?'

Something tender about the question makes him drift off himself, perhaps the weary melancholy that turned her voice down low. It's the first time she's used his name in conversation. Fifty times last night, but that was urgent, this clamorous lover. Not noise, he reminds himself, remembering his alarm, just sound, up loud. He sees his father's fading face and is at once secure; his mother leans into the picture and says something tart but fair.

'Yeah. The messing up was done at school.'

He carries the forfeit in silence on one side, an eardrum lost to discipline. The deaf ear entails some explanation, technical terms, like pairing off.

'Pairing off?'

He explains the punishment drill. You stood face to face with another culprit – say your shoes weren't clean or you were out of step – and at a word from the prefect you began slapping each other. Every now and then he'd call out *harder!* and you had to jack it up or he came and showed you how. Pairing off spared him the trouble. It was all right if you were with a friend: there were ways of making the slaps resound, like cupping the hand.

'But if you got an enemy it could get rough.'

'Barbaric!'

'No, just boarding school, old style.'

He's trying to convey that that wasn't the worst of it, though it left the most permanent mark. The other, wider torment never ceased. This was just an accident, a session with a hard case that burst the eardrum. And taught a lesson, so who said you learnt nothing at school? You learnt that the species is hierarchical and incorrigible and will trump you at every step. So you had better find an ally you can trust.

'I guess it worked,' he clarifies. 'So talk on my right side.'

They're still looking at the painting on the screen.

'Her feet are almost out of the picture,' Aline nods, 'and his are almost in. He's supposed to be untroubled, he has no *Guernica*, no politics. But he has his marriage and Marguerite.'

'She looks scary.'

'Maybe. She looks a bit like Red.' She laughs. 'I'm sort of scared of *her*!'

'It's the way she's almost toppling out of the picture. Like she could swallow you up, a black hole.'

'Well, he took her on. You know, X would have denied paternity, Y would pay her keep, Z would go missing, but Matisse makes a picture of her, the beautiful problem. Every picture was a problem to be solved. You sort of wonder: how did the transfer take place? Did Caroline, that's the first woman, not want the encumbrance? Anyhow, she's gone her way and he's married now. All this is running through his head as he sketches. He looks at his family. Wife knitting, boys dozing: they are now. Marguerite is *then*, when he was free. He wants both.'

She looks at Zach. How can he know what that entails? The bachelor wants a family, the family man wants to be free: Matisse knows that now; it's the central fact of his life and it's worth all the experiments he performs in that lab at the bottom of the garden, all the gleanings in the Louvre, all the goadings every time young Picasso comes around, all the fancy notions of relativity in the air, all the theory, theory, theory. This is practice. When he puts its tensions into the painting he can demolish distance and free time and set every last brown spot dancing.

F ace 2

Drunk Phuljari hurries down the nightblack road.

He has a wall eye, from a firecracker accident when he was a child. It's stony and dead, but when he's upset it bucks and skips and rolls up to the sky. Right now it's jumping like fried eggwhite. He's dribbling too. He'll show the bastards. His smudge – *his* smudge! – and they debar him. Who cased the joint, marked the gate? Who made discreet enquiries, found out the owners were away, abroad? He, Phuljari!

It was just face. Nag trying to save his.

That punk Gilgitan gets away with murder and I cop it! I who live by the rules, even help make them. First he takes something bigger than a hand, then he won't sell it and split the cash. And the fence offering six hundred bucks when he heard which house it was from! Says the painting's lost, it fell out of his langot as he ran. I say share and share alike, that's the first law of blackshorts, or you drop out. Lots of other work if you really want it. But what does old Nagface do? Turns on me! Says he smells grog on me and won't have it. What am I doing drunk on the job, he wants to know. What's Paltaniya going to say? And the goddess? As if she'd grudge me a nip, and Paltaniya drunk all day.

RED

Then when we've eaten and I see the lamp is burning down and get up to trim the wick he starts his palaver. Leave the wick alone, who needs light anyway, the meat was oversalted, did we ever find a stash of notes like this in Paltaniya's day, and if any motherfucker wants to fight let him say so. Not looking anyone in the eye, especially not Gilgitan. I go ahead and trim the wick anyway or we'll all be in darkness and when I look at the glass I'm so shocked by what I read there I almost drop the lantern. The soot says, and when did soot lie, goddess, goddess, my mouth goes all dry and I need a swig of something quick, the soot says, so naturally I turn to them, to all present, isn't that my duty as secretary, do I ever grudge young Vinod his job as treasurer, but I have to speak because the soot says, I don't shout it naturally, someone is going to die.

Then they all jump on me, the bastards, for speaking the truth as I see it, for warning them, and Nag looks hard at me and says, right, no smudge for you, Phuljari, you skip a turn, we can manage without you at the next job since you can't manage without liquor, you know the rules.

Just face.

G *is for* G ipsy

See also G ilgitan, G ecko,
   G oddess

G ipsy *also* **Rom, Dom,** groups turned nomadic after Aryan ascendancy; outcastes, with subcastes such as blacksmiths, knife grinders, pole-vaulters, bear-tamers, and horse thieves.

G ecko the house lizard; sleek, timid, yellowish indoor creature, hides behind pictures, content with a frame, but can fight spirited territorial battles and lose a tail, which regrows (*see* **Narrator**); contrast the free-ranging garden lizard or **Gilgitan**.

G ilgitan the red or garden lizard, or chameleon; changes colour from grey to green to red, hence its common name, 'bloodsucker'; not to be confused with the house lizard, the **Gecko**, to whom it stands somewhat in the relation of freeman to slave. Seldom longer than twelve inches, with fierce aspect that owes something to its hackles, a serrated ridge of spinal hair, and its unforgiving eyes in which there burns an ancient fury; flat lower jaw, detachable for swallowing prey larger than the head, tight lips, black tongue, ears little more than a hole in the head (but unlike the gecko's light does not show through); long wiry tail, supple limbs, widespread toes of which the great toe bends all the way back, digits suckered but also clawed for climbing trees, walls, etc.

Gilgitan the man; born a Bansberia, the pole-vaulter

subcaste among Doms, father a pole-vaulter, mother of the bear-tamer subcaste (monkey dancer on her mother's side); education, government school till age eleven; has been in his thirty-odd years:

1. a tumbler and vaulter
2. a miner
3. a tyre retreader's airfiller
4. a truck driver (has an expired licence, forged)
5. a truck painter, a sundry painter
6. a drain layer
7. a tiler's assistant

G oddess 1

When Sethji's new truck is finished, the paintings on the flat-work, right up to the eagle and the peacock on the fascia, there is still one blank space Gilgitan can fill. It is the face of the diesel tank by the rear wheel: black, rectangular, smooth sheet steel, a new surface for the brush. Just to feel the difference after the grained wood of the tailgate (the HORN PLEASE filigreed above, arabesques below separating OK from TA-TA) and the side panel-ling, a pair of Kashmir lake scenes, one on each side. The lakes kept him singing under his breath, the same four-note refrain that always possesses him when he is sad, and left him with a distant focus to his eyes when he came out of the frame.

Why do you hide your face, goddess, why do I never see you?

If he listened he would hear her answer. When have I ever hidden my face? I was the tea you drank this morning by the sugarcane field. Remember how I steamed over the green tips of the cane, how gratefully you swallowed me? How I sweetened your tongue, warmed the innards of you, caressed you all the way down?

But he's sulking, so the answer is drowned in the shifting gears as he decides he will throw in one painting free.

Free, Sethji! This one's for nothing.

And Sethji laughs as much as to say, go on then, waste my paint. You seem to have all the time in the world. Some of us have work to do. And pushes off.

So Gillu turns to face the black rectangle, stares at it, grows sombre. The old sad song returns unbidden like a work chant and his lips move as he mouths the refrain. *When will you show your face?* He lifts a hand and draws with his little finger, no chalk. Let the diesel filler pipe be in the design, its chrome cap a sun gleaming over the landscape. Hills, naturally, a house, a path. Trees straight as pencils, with that seductive pointed-arch top, bushes bush-shaped. A river, no lake, long low boat, one oar. Reeds, lotuses, a fish jumping. A grassed way with a bullock cart, a woman.

(This one he'll spend time on, all day tomorrow: Sethji's young wife looks like she wants to feed him. Put her in. One hand raised to her nose ring, the other holding the pallu of her sari taut over her hair, oiled, neatly parted, done up in a bun behind. Brass pot on her head, mouth like a ripe fig.)

The hills go on first, straight green, but dry darker as the background black shows through. He dips the brush in red for the house roof and finds it hurts the eye, then mixes in too much black so lightens it with white and delights in the resulting rose. Trees, bushes, reeds grow up, a path appears winding along beside the blue-black river. What bullock cart? The boat's enough. Now the woman. (No lunch, sister, today's my fast.) Her face goes from full front with nose jewel to three-quarter to profile and still it's not right. Let her face the other way, just the outline of her cheek. No bun, let the hair hang down over her shoulders. The sari pallu spreads into a snake hood, the paisley sari pattern coils

into the spectacles-mark on a cobra. Good. Now her husbands.
Sethji first, in sadhu weeds, then four others, langot-clad. The last
lagging behind a bit. There. The family.

The chrome diesel filler cap rides above the landscape, a moon.
As he lowers the brush it strikes the pipe. A spray of white
speckles the sky.

Stars.

G oddess 2

'*Great Hera help me!*': I can still see Wonder Woman's nervous frown from my Marvel comic book as she prepares to face another foe. How I shadowed her, how I coveted that Teflon skin! How could I know I would marry her? That I would lie beside the same blue-black hair, the identical Juno chin of my own goddess of worry? Half-Aztec this one, but Wonder Woman's very double, from unmussable sweep of hair to perfect sandalled feet. But what it is to bed perfection only the imperfect know; the breathless pleasures, the wonderment and disbelief, the spooked apnoea of waking into nothing. What she saw in me I cannot imagine. Unless it was that Olivia was immune to every danger but worship, and I, out of old habit, adored that stern lithop beauty until she succumbed. Even now when she is far away and in someone else's bed I have only to cup my hands and her perfect face is there –

here look!

– so palpably here that I know it has vanished at the other end of the world, causing horror and derangement in her partner of the moment.

Again: *look!*

RED

Olivia.

See? Perhaps I have at last some small share in Wonder Woman's powers, perhaps even power, this fleeting power, over Wonder Woman.

H *is for* H eart

See also H ome, H ousepride

H eart

In the dream I open the door to my chest, step in, and shut it behind me. Inside me it is spacious and cold, not especially dark but not bright. In the half light I notice my organs lumped together, packed like meats on a walk-in freezer shelf. They take up surprisingly little space; I would have thought they'd fill the cavity of me but they are stacked neatly one upon the other as if to leave room for me to walk around in. I could be in the basement of a tower with pipes and ducting and a whiff of diesel. The heart glistens dark red, a lubricant on its surface reflecting a white striplight down some corridor. It is throbbing, weakly. Other organs in other shades – the liver is puce, the kidneys raw umber – and different shapes – the kidneys are shiny boxing gloves – go about their business routinely, a pulse, a blip, an occasional flutter, but the heart insists on this feeble, almost reproachful toiling. You have done this to me, it is saying.

The dream occurs during a phase when people, doctors and family, are advising a bypass. For my own good. Whereas I value the integrity of my unbreached person. For a while I go about more than usually aware of my breastbone; in hardware stores my eye will rest on the bright edge of a disc saw before moving on. During this phase I find myself looked at differently by those in the know; then I stop noticing.

Years ago a quarrel with the Aztec drove me out of the house in a rage. It was a summer's night and as I walked uphill into a warm dry wind I began to feel a pain in my chest. Pain, wind, and gradient brought me to a standstill. I stood there in the dark marvelling at the strange twisted thudding in my chest, as if a towel wrapped around my heart were being wrung.

The episode passed. A year later my doctor (until then I had never thought of a doctor as mine) sent me to a specialist whose tests indicated heart disease. An angiogram showed the chief vessel supplying the heart, the left anterior descending artery, which I came to call by its affectionate medical acronym, the LAD, to be 90% blocked.

90%! You are appalled. But not for long: after all, you are immortal. Before the angiogram I was required to sign a form which stated my awareness of the risks of the procedure, some 1% chance of death. I signed with the smiling gravitas of one who has never been in hospital before. Only a clear sentence of death, probably not even that, can persuade a man to take his death seriously. What you do begin to take more seriously is your life. Not that you took it lightly before. It was and remains the mystery of mysteries, but you do grow more regardful of it – until you return to living as before, without the cocked ear that is worse than any gun.

Chekhov travelled through Siberia with a bad heart and felt as fit as ever. Back home he heard an erratic beat and, a doctor himself, read his doom. No doubt he changed certain habits and began to write with a new urgency, but the consciousness killed him. Irregular beats do cause alarm. Every fourth beat missed means a quarter less blood going around; every third beat missed and you feel distinctly faint. When it's down to every other beat you concentrate marvellously. After all, at that point you're half dead. In the heart of that silence the death you carried inside you has begun audibly to stir. Then even that realization passes.

There is another, more cruel, dream that comes around. In it I am cured of my disease. Nothing can touch me now in this new radiance: my heart beats normally and will do so forever. The dream and the ecstasy it brings goes on and on, like the most exquisite slip on the unglazed pot of my sleeping self: I can feel myself smiling even as I wake up.

Think of the heart: concentrate on it, picture it in every mundane detail. In the era of the image it's no longer iconic; everyone knows what a real heart looks like: the familiar wallet of flesh in a mesh of arteries. For centuries men heard it and felt its beat and wondered, imagining shapes for it, and settling on the red one in the pack of cards. The real thing, bulbous, asymmetrical, is always a disappointment, a spitting toad, where we hoped for a prince.

At first you begin to step more lightly. You begin to hold yourself delicately, differently. At the same time you begin to live more freely. Morning tinglings alarm you. You know statistically that attacks occur more often in the morning. You know the heart is complaining. Feed me. So you feed it, almonds, honey, then any fruit at hand. This inchfruit left out to ripen under a napkin. It's ready. The hexagons of rind are coming away. I eat an inch, all I can take of the scent anyway, a scent that says Vietnam, Southeast Asia, Elsewhere. Not home.

H ome where your finger finds the light switch unerringly
in the dark

Comes a mail to my home computer:

> E
> [from my middle name]
> *Just a thought.* [I sit up. She's been plotting]
> *Would you like to see Manda? Strikes me you don't really
> know each other.*
> O

Do I know my daughter? No. I just know her handwriting.
Wide spaces between the lines.

H ousepride

Window grilles are worst. Between every set of iron bars is a secure trench for dirt. Lint scrolls in that angleiron well, dust settles there, hair and scales of skin bed down in that canyon, asbestos fibrils, hepatitis germs, motes, mites, mothwings, atoms of passing asteroids, gecko droppings, all find there a secure staging post before resuming, twenty years from now, or ten, their passage down the scale of matter. Spiders will pitch their tents down there and simply abandon them, profligate with silk; morning mosquitoes, looking for a way out to light, testing every square in the wire mesh for size, snag in the rigging and die epic deaths, dry to husks by nightfall, and turn to dust, more dust. To get between the bars and the mesh you need a long staple flathead half-inch brush, and you must simply flick since there's no scope for lifting, painstaking work, well by iron well between the bars.

For surely any trace of dirt would offend this miracle of an American daughter.

She's on her way! Well, there's still six weeks, the rest of her term at school, and then she has some singing competition. But her room must be perfect, windows reglazed and puttied, sanded, primered, painted. And that's just windows. The whole house to be turned inside out and shaken, nothing – no mould or roach – that might put off this blood-of-my-bone alien, coming home.

I *is for* I nterruptus

See also I ntimus, I gnis fatuus

I nterruptus

'Look, music is music, performance is in another building, OK?'

That's the director's last word: her hands part expressively, palms outermost like a dancer parting the Red Sea. She's lost her cool and spoken abruptly, a harassed woman this week.

Zach who has been trying to fuse the two arts in his head thought he might sneak a prop onstage with the musicians, a mattress. After all if last night's performance man could use music while sawing slabs out of a styrofoam gizzard in his Meat is Murder apron and smearing them with barbecue sauce, what's a mattress? Admittedly in another building.

'But go ahead, what the hell.' She's back, the director. 'Am I chief legislator for the arts?' Smiling.

So the lights come up on twenty musicians, six from the Indian consulate, and a mattress. Queen-sized, from the Sorsa company of Finland who want no posters on the proscenium, just their logo on the programme, a mountain with its head in a cloud. It's just a loan; they get the mattress back.

Even for a small auditorium it's a low turnout. Officials in the front row, then their invitees in the second, then a yawning red mouth of plush empty seats. The idle and curious singly and in pairs along either side like uneven teeth, and a knot of students at the very back, at the tonsils. One raffish group hog the middle, on both sides of the aisle, occupying two and three seats each, octopus legs hung over the row ahead. Young, dyed hair, black-and-steel glints. Menacing in the way of a beached colony of Portuguese men-of-war, insouciant in the way of corals and sea cucumbers under the ocean's wash.

The strings have just launched the diminished key that signals a change of heart in the queen. Heads tilt as guests of the officials check the narrative in their programmes. When two slurred syllables rise into the middle air and ping off the Tsarist chandeliers.

'Bo-ring!'

The voice is American, from the front of that spiky black-and-steel gothic lot in the middle. Officials turn in their seats and frown, giggles from the students at the back.

'*Boring!*'

More clearly this time. Calmly stated, law.

Titters from the audience as necks crane to see the truthteller. So far all has been frosty politeness. It's a girl wrapped in a black mantilla, yawning noisily. She has her green boots up on the seat in front of her and she begins a slow clap which her friends take up. One or two further down in the audience join in. The girl gets up and saunters down the aisle. Studies the cellist at close quarters, makes a mock bow to the concert master, wanders past the fiddles to the steps which she mounts with her hands folded behind her. Dull moons faded in the seat of her low-slung black jeans; red line of lace above.

It's *her*!

Her friends are on their feet now, strolling down the aisle, jongleurs from the Dark Ages of some galactic future. One is on a unicycle – they took it for a wheelchair at the door; one is juggling particoloured bean balls. With a magic word Zach stays the director, who's jumped to her feet to protest.

'Aleatoric,' he whispers, 'right?'

It's her! It's bleeding her! The salvia-red hair, the black mantilla, the black silk nightie worn bustier-fashion over gauze wedding sleeves. Litmus-pink translucent skin, so bony she could be anorexic. With a gang of slashers on crack. Hair bound up in stooks, those commando boots; her museum outfit. It's like she's following him and not the other way around.

The director looks vinegar at Zach over rimless glasses but can fabricate a smile. Still, she has a responsibility to the musicians who are soldiering on with bewildered concentration. Keep going, she signs to the concert master, whose fiercely angled chin reassures the orchestra. Munshi Manohar Lal of the Gorakhpur gharana spanks his tabla into submission; he's been on the circuit long enough to expect the worst of whites. They never disappoint, his glance tells tanpura master Bir Singh, who bought his music diploma six weeks ago in Jalandhar. Singh fingers air and follows the black-whites' antics closely. They're not disrupting anything; they're now sprawled onstage in attitudes of listening, as if they simply needed to get closer to the music. Even the juggler is looking for a tempo among the circling balls while the cyclist gyros onstage, head bent, chin on fist, like the Thinker.

Red has begun a sluttish snake dance from out of Rimsky-Korsakov (Zach recognizes the theft is his own and blushes to see it publicly announced) around the mattress. Her lover, a real-life flautist, is sulking with his back to her, engrossed in the shehnai, while Zach, whose good ear was returning to the melody, rewriting it as he does while listening, is distracted once more. A moment ago he'd thought to welcome the intruders with his arms thrown open, but now he stands again, takes up the ektara beside the concertmaster, and begins to bow its single wire. She's astride the mattress now, one foot on either side, looking back at him as if she knows his fate. It's about fucking, isn't it, Mr Composeur? her smug eyes say. No, he wants to answer, you stunning cunt, it's about killing. Instead he leaves off bowing and turns to plucking the sad single string stretched across the frail clay cup. He plucks with a tinny banjo-like note in time with the tread of her greendaub boots. The taut brown soundbox paper, the kind he covered schoolbooks with, lends the pizzicato a crêpe-papery air that shifts the galumphing jackboot tread into an approaching horse, making four legs plus the unicyclist's one. She sees and steps lightly now, bending over backwards under the whinny, so when she sinks down on her back, legs locked apart, the whole flank of the beast is there, its black shimmering with flecks of colour like rubbed granite. The music ends, her jilted lover stands, stretches, hangs menace over her so she stabs upward, he rears and falls.

All saw a horse die, right?

I ntimus

He's pissed off, Alex, her lover, and stomped out in his Doc Martins, the ones she brought him, the bastard, calling her an exhibitionist bitch, he can talk, fucker. She looks up at Zach from her corner seat in the auditorium where the rest left her when she refused to budge, kitehigh and trembling, seeing and not seeing, recognizing him through one slit in her defences, the one she fires arrows through when the drug's much less bright than now. He's the Indian guy, slick, who wrote that shit her body was up there gyrating to twenty million years ago. So what's he want? Doesn't everybody, from her? His mouth squared off like some picaro in a Spanish story, his face growing flat as a screen, blank with just a cursor, going onoffonoff in his eye when he comes up close to say *You OK?* Then it withdraws to the far far horizon high above the low blue hills from where it beams:

'*Not* boring!'

Delivered like sunlight, bright to blinding but impartial, as if the judgement concerned neither of them, composer and interruptress. Smiling but. So since everybody's gone home, audience and musicians and Alex and them, she stands carefully and takes his arm and finds she can walk. The Hilton she knows, has stayed there when she got here once before her mother and couldn't get into the mews, so it could be her own room not his she finds herself in. You know, she says, sitting on the carpet with her back against the bed, sipping the flat soda he put in her hand, it was really really interesting the way the horse, and then she loses her thread and starts in again, the way the horse. Giggling then at the futility of it, all of it, even this comforting hand she has half a mind to bite, hard, and half a mind to kiss. So lets him do what he seems to want to do, the usual, even undoes a button on him, with stops for breath and unlacing, and one for a story of how yesterday she was in this laundromat she goes to for kicks right across the Pont Neuf from the Louvre just to watch the clothes go round and round in the dryers, more random than a kaleido-scope, less predictable than TV, until she falls asleep in the telling so the last thing she remembers is he's laying her out, clothed, untouched, feet together like a dead queen.

I gnis fatuus

The house is at the edge of the village, hard by the forest. It was Phuljari who picked up the scent, scouted around, left a bent twig pointing at the gate, so he had every right to come, but he was drunk and Nag debarred him. He then got every back up, even those who thought His Snakeship highhanded, by predicting someone was going to die.

It's the dark night of the moon, but even in the bright fortnight the men would be hard to see in their blacking. They walk in silence a little behind His Snakeship, ready to melt into the canefields at the first sound of a car or truck. They have been along this road earlier in the week, in checked lungis, so they looked like Andhra labourers. At the agricultural college they leave the road and go all the way around the campus boundary wall into the fields in case the nightwatchman at the gate is up. In the chickpea field they fall into single file walking along a bund. Where they turn left at the corner of a stand of cane Gilgitan stops to piss off the edge, spraying to make it quieter. When it's chilly like this you're forever pissing, he thinks, sniffing at the fenugreeky odour to the urine. He tweaks the hose to choke the spray and pretends to initial the turned sod in yellow ink. G. Old friend dick, none closer: sleeps in the cup of his left hand.

Straight ahead bulks a small square cell that could be a pumphouse. Gilgitan darts along the bund to investigate, his sure feet gripping the crabgrass. It's a plain brick shelter, one room, too old to be the pumphouse he was expecting. A simple chain that fastens the door at the lintel and he undoes it to look inside. Just a room filled with straw and firewood where a farmer might spend a night. Smell of straw and rat dirt. It would be a good place to bring the pig girl, he thinks as he catches up with the rest. They're always looking for a rooting place. She has the whitest teeth he's seen. He'll bring her here and take her and take her and make her his bitch. On a night like this when it's black as the Mother and only her slant eyes and her canines point to where the rest of her is. God! He feels the rush of blood as his cock lengthens. What else *is* there, really? Really, really, really? New potatoes in fenugreek, the night sky, and the smell of a woman's part. And then you're finished, like the pig, your throat cut.

He snatches up a handful of green chickpeas and runs back along the bund to catch up with the file. These smudges he can take or leave, maybe the first two were fun. Will it be like that with her? After the first few times she'll want to marry him. He sees his free life suddenly boxed in. Why are they like that? When he's with a woman he gives himself completely, holds nothing back. She is his goddess, he's nothing. The pig bitch, now, she's a beauty; he loves every inch of her. Only she can soothe the prickles he feels under a sky like this one, this wide black expanse he must love as well as fear because there are nights when he steps outside simply to be reminded. She soothes also the terrible kicks in the ass the city gives you. Puts herself in between, this little woman. In her arms he knows there is nothing he would not give her. He loves her more than anything he can think of, more than he loves himself for sure, and what could he love more than that? He loves her and then he goes on his way. Why can't she go on hers?

His feet leave grass and dust and climb the berm with its loose gravel. The detour has brought the men out on the main road short of the electric transformer; the house is a little way past the cross roads behind a row of silver oaks.

High overhead in the dark a row of ducks quacks twice, speeding like an invisible arrow. Gilgitan glances up at the heavens as he steps back onto the metalled road. The sky is a powdery black, soft and furrowed like the lampblack in the bowl, with wriggling blue spiders that come spinning down on threads. But the brightest star in the sky, straight up above the house, is red.

Mars is closer to the Earth tonight than at any time in the past 73,000 years, the TV says. Big figures like that make him uneasy. Gilgitan lets his eyes linger on its shimmering watery surface; how many hours would it take a spacecraft to reach there? The red star seems to wink at him, to want to say something, and a shiver goes down his back. The nights are still bearable, thank god; deep winter smudges are hard tack. But then the roads are bare, even of dogs, and neighbours snug in their quilts. You don't even think of getting caught. For that matter you don't in summer either; if you started it'd end up coming true.

'Tsss.'

His Snakeship pats the air beside him and they wake up and step softly. They come to the gate Phuljari marked. It's a foot entrance directly in front of the house; cars must go around the back. One high step up from the road, a flat rock, the gate wrought iron. A brass name plate Gilgitan, the only reader, fingers. It's too dark to make out anything.

The shingle path leads through crotons growing in the ground to a deep veranda that slopes around three sides of the house. A white tubelight at the eaves saps the red in the shoe flower bushes on either side of the front step and leaves the rest of the veranda in a darkness seeded with neon fog.

They force the door and step over the threshold one by one. Huddle in the doorway, each man alone among the house ghosts. And then, just as their eyes are opening to the dark, they hear a sound. A rancorous on and off muttering like a tuning knob being twiddled on a radio. It's somewhere near at hand in a tone known elsewhere but hidden by the double darkness of night and new surroundings.

It's right behind them.

Phuljari stumbles up the stone step at the gate, cursing under his rattlesome phlegmy breath, walking with the steady tread of the conscientious drunk straight up the path to the shadows of the veranda. The men inside freeze.

'Mother!' Nag whispers the challenge from the door.

'Wife!' is the password – they learnt this from Paltaniya – but it doesn't come to Phuljari's slow tongue.

Nag jumps him with the double strength of fear. But luck and darkness preserve a drunk. Phuljari weaves away from the lunge and smells His Snakeship's hair oil go by. He brings his fist down like a hammer and connects right on the back of the neck. Nag's chin hits the floor at an absurd angle and he lies where he fell, his neck broken.

O my god you mad motherfucker what have you gone and done! Phuljari is sobering up quickly but the hooch fug just won't clear right out. Something tells him, the way the man fell, the way he went still, the way he still won't move, the way he turns over when shaken, something's badly wrong, that he's done for for good and ever and is never going to move again, and he, Phuljari, did it. The men see who it is now, come out into the veranda.

Someone was going to die, someone was going to die, now he remembers. But who would have said he, Phuljari, would be the killer!

Gilgitan keeps his head when the others are for running.

'Madmen! He's in uniform. What happens when they find him here tomorrow oiled and blacked and in shorts? They come looking for us, right?' He grabs Nag under the arms and drags him into the house. In there he checks for a pulse, lays his head across the chest to listen for the faintest murmur at the heart. But it's clear the man's dead.

'Here, you check again, Phuljari.'

But Phuljari won't come near Nag. The others take turns at checking the pulse. Not a trace. They all saw the way the head rolled when Gilgitan moved the body.

'Candles,' Gilgitan calls to no one in particular, 'there'll be some in the kitchen.'

When the light comes he takes down a curtain and carefully wipes Nag's body. Leaves the langot in place, wipes on either side of the bulge, down the inner thigh, around the buttock, down each warm leg. When he's done, he removes the langot, looking the other way when the clout falls off. Other men's dicks he hates.

'Newspapers,' he says, 'any paper.'

Already the men sense they are following orders. Phuljari goes looking, anything to get away from where Nag's death fills the room.

'Not books, idiot,' Gilgitan hisses at Chhanga, but does not go in search as he would have before. He stands there looking at Nag in the candlelight, so newly dead, so surely dead. The face says: defunct. There's nothing to prepare you for this emptying, nothing in all the slow spoiling that life brings to features, to prepare you for this look of exhausted idiocy. Nag's dead. There are green chickpeas in the fields and he's dead.

Vinod comes in with an armful of newspapers he found in the storeroom.

'Scrunch them up under the dining table,' Gilgitan says without stirring. Chhanga, anxious to make amends, has brought in some kindling from the garden and tents the twigs over the hived paper.

'Where's Phuljari?'

He's been standing back in the doorway, neither in nor out, but knows he can't get away with it and comes forward out of the shadows.

'Take the feet. Vinod, help him.'

They lift Nag onto the dining table. When he is laid out each one bids him goodbye in his own way; Phuljari simply stands apart with his eyes shut and his hands folded, swaying. Then Gilgitan touches the candle to the pyre. The paper is slow to catch so he balls the soiled curtain and tosses it onto the flame. The fabric blazes up instantly and the twigs ignite. Chhanga lays the chairs down so the legs stick into the flames.

'Here, this end,' Gilgitan directs him to the head. Presently the tabletop is engulfed and Nag's hair flames up. Black hair of his vanity.

'Come on,' Phuljari begs, and no one's for staying. But Gilgitan holds up a hand. He goes up close to check the blistering face. He will never again use black and red in his paintwork without being reminded of this moment. But all present understand now the face must be erased, and all know why the eyes must fry to nothing.

J *is for* J ail

At first the jail walls cling to him like the clothes of a madman. He shuts his eyes against them, looks up at the sky, down at the ground, at his hands, at the wings of his nose, at anything that is not wall, especially the banyan tree. But its patience disturbs him. The crows in it are a source of comfort; he listens attentively to their conversation, hangs on the slightest aberration in their habits or grooming. One has a club foot and he follows its progress. Sparrows he watches in a way he never bothered to outside, the way they fluff out their modest feathers, roll in the dust and refuse larger concerns. By night the fruit bats simply drop in from heaven.

Men he is wary of. They could be informers, they are certainly of caste, and would pull it, even in here. Best give a neutral name, his father taught him.

When the guards admitted him he confessed to Gillu but clearly that was not enough.

'Full name, donkey.'

'Gilgit.'

'Gilgit is a place, oaf.'

'The same. My father came from there.'

'Hindu or Mussalman?'

'Is there any difference?'

Slap!

He gives his caste as knifegrinder and learns to hold his tongue. It's not his first time: he's been in and out. Straight in after government school. Out is better but you learn things in here and the food could be worse. This time he learns vegetable gardening, a grid, rows, pegged string, little labels on twigs stuck in the earth. The rake he likes, the sifting, levelling, sorting, as he wonders who dobbed him in, but mostly the rocking weight and balance of it in his hands, almost a pole. He still can't stomach routine, but even the flying foxes have times they keep to in the grainy dark.

Just as the evening light is failing they appear high in the sky, so high tonight they seemed to emerge from the tip of the horned moon. Soft as soot they beat a calm track across the dusk looking neither right nor left, always singly. They travel clear across the sky and vanish into the twilight as if bound for some other world – and suddenly: there they are in the tree, this banyan tree outside the dormitory window, hanging upside down, feeding. He listens to their khitter phitter, so mousy and mundane after the measured silence of their vampire flight.

The pig girl he meditates on until one night she appears. He's staring at the cracks in the whitewash when suddenly they begin to heave and two nipples appear and the breasts behind them, and her nose and her knees and toes and then the whole face and the round belly of her as she steps through the wall. Not all the way in: the cunt of her is buried in plaster.

'Are you letting that horse rider in?' he asks, surprised by possessiveness.

'This is yours,' she points, but keeps it hidden.

'So who squealed?'

'Phuljari.'

'Bastard. I'll fix him.'

'No, you won't. He's dead.'

'She got him!'

Gilgitan's shaken. They both know who he means. The goddess, who hunts down her husband's killer.

'How?'

'He fell down the steps behind Basheer's saloon. He had just had a haircut and paid in cash.'

'You have the painting?'

'It's here.' Again the finger points between her legs. 'Do you want it?'

'Keep it warm for me.'

Then she's gone, the black of her melting away into the cracks of the limewash, the faintest snatch of red where her four limbs cross.

K *is for* K ama

See also K angra, K alam

Kangra the Himalayan school of miniature painting, after the town of that name

> 'What Chinese art accomplished for landscape is here achieved for human love.'
>
> Ananda Coomaraswamy

> '...adulterers, who love each other with real love'
>
> Pablo Neruda

The lovers are in a forest. Her husband is away selling ginger and alum, his wife burns midnight oil and in the morning walks with her hair hanging loose to the temple.

They have spread a mat of leaves. Overhead a banana tree unfurls one tender green flag that falls into the silence, shudders once, and goes still. Dew, tense as a maiden, calm as glass, deep as crystal, casts its thousand eyes up to heaven; the sun bares its teeth but cannot reach in here. 'My little sister, Roll Up Your Eyes, who prays forty minutes to my twenty, was saying I'll come back (meaning me, not her) as a worm if I see you again.' 'Tell her to mind god's business or I'll show her what.' 'What?' 'This.' 'You men.' The afternoon ripens. A breeze comes fingering the new banana leaf; the leaf shivers and stops its mouth with a small green fist. In this climate the peaches fall before they go pink so pick them yellow and let them ripen in the bowl. One breast now

159

bare, she feeds him green almonds one by one, letting every third one slip between her own teeth. Where is his other hand? He is wearing the usual garment loosely tied. His flute lies forgotten under a fig, but never again will she hear a single woodwind note without her heart turning over. One swollen fruit has split open along its seams while yet clinging to its stalk, hidden from the pigeon by the modest leaf. Only the golden ants have found it: how blithely they range over the exposed sweetness as if they had for ever in that purple twilight! She has painted her nails red for him, something she omits to do for the merchant. He has freshened his mouth with anise. Darkly he lifts her onto the stem of him. Light as a spinning top she turns so the babblers in the mango tree stop their babbling and stare. Moss green velvets the rain-drunk earth, hyacinths dot the pond. Bled purple the clock-vine flowers on his forehead, brilliant the poppy of her fallen skirts. Is that cloud or a flamingo?

Is the artist a mere colourist? No, notice how his line leads you: the trunk of the mango he lends to the man's foot as a brace, all nature the lovers' trestle. Do the leaves mirror his hands, the fruit her breasts or not? Witness the sly latticework of branches that reveals and conceals the lovers' parts. And who is that peering through the cheetah's human eyes if not the returning husband? Why do the black clouds on the horizon tear their open tresses if not for crying out loud? And what will we say of the serpent lightnings in the strip of stormy sky that leap the block of text into folio 12?

K ama love

Never such a dawn
sky a bruised indigo in that window
where cypress treetops cringe to remember last night's
    contortions
and here the other way a blush that says
the fierce lightnings the rain the thunder
were simply allies keeping the alum wallah away
for one last night as my true lord lay here
above me and under and everywhere at once in the dark
the doors shut tight that stand open now
and the sad blue light that bathes the forecourt
was black and endless

in a minute the sun will show
his hateful face the servants theirs
grindstone dust and gossip burst in
to anneal the heart encaust every swollen sense
stamp out desire and turn to ashes any remnant of bliss

but for now this pale blue interval these birdcalls

that have never failed to calm the spirit
and these nailmarks

here   and   here

                        and

                        here

K alam pen

The last folio, folio 17, tells a story. A certain painter went to the king and said, Your Highness, give me work. The king said, Paint then my queen. The painter prostrated himself and fetched his paints. He was blindfolded and led into the harem. There the Abyssinian eunuch presented him to the queen saying, The king would have this man paint you. That is my wish too, said the queen, for I have heard of this painter. It is said the birds peck at the custard apples in his paintings and squirrels gnaw at his pomegranates. That's as may be, Your Majesty, said the eunuch and withdrew. Leave us, said the queen and her maids obeyed. The queen unveiled her beauty and turned to the painter, saying, Begin. Daily the painter was brought into her presence and daily his painting grew. Witchcraft, whispered the maids when they saw her majesty imprisoned within the borders of the painting as in a magic mirror. The man grew so bold as to turn up the corners of her mouth at the ends. The queen obliged by matching his painted smile with a smile of her own. The king noted these smiles. The painter then gave her small hands and feet but she despaired of matching those. Finally he drew a pair of spectacles on her nose. The queen was distraught, but the next day she sent for the British resident and had him order a pair of spectacles. When the glasses arrived she discovered the joy of clear vision. The king showered gold on the prescient painter and sent him away with a fresh assignment. He was to paint from imagination a picture of the queen as the beautiful Radha awaiting her lord Krishna in the bedchamber. The king would carry this painting close to his heart when he was far from home. The painter went home with a light step and flung himself into his work. Some days it seemed he could draw with his eyes closed, so deep did he go into the painting of his life. For the first time he laid aside all rules, all the tenets of his painter forefathers. When the work was done he made a final break with tradition and signed the painting. As he was returning the pen to its tray a black droplet fell on the page. The next day he returned to court with the commission. The king paled at the sight of his painted queen. Scoundrel! he cried, and had the man clapped in irons. For the king had noticed a mole painted on the inner thigh exactly where his beloved had one. How could the painter have known? He banished the queen to the remote fortress of Chamba and undertook a pilgrimage to the holy lake of Mansarowar without any painting in his heart pocket. The painter was given one copper coin, blinded with an ink pen, and set to breaking stones on the new road to Chamba. And all mimetic art was henceforth forbidden in the kingdom. This was the story.

L *is for* L ove

L ove

The box of chocolates she buzz-bombs burns gold on the glass table. A ravaged city losing just its truffle darks to her strategic hand. She knows the score in the unequal wargame, watches her blood sugar soar like fireworks over Coney Island. One foot on the cauldron of the potted bayleaf, one in the tiled blue shallows of her rooftop pool, her runners steaming, towelling socks balled and July ripe. Looking out over the Hudson, seeing only the Neva, turning up the same Jack over and over in the pack of images she brought home last night over the Atlantic. High over Greenland she looked down once at midnight, straight down into the jaws of hell, ice without end.

Chocolate helps, or doesn't hurt, its smallest elements soothe and excite at once like amphetamines in the blood. Right now a Hazchem truck of neurotoxins is overturned at the busy intersection of the vagus and the whole jangling web of nerves that is Aline Medlar in love.

To: Zaccheus W
Sender: Aline M

>Back in NY last night, heart not among luggage, soul

arriving by unscheduled flight in Dariya Dun. Do you have an airport (just kidding) or must it crash land and die within hailing distance of you? Where's home? I used the NASA atlas to zoom in on your valley but couldn't see your place. Their camera picks up streams and canals and fallen matchsticks. What's your house like? Is there an address, like a number on the gate? Are you on the phone? Couldn't take Peter without you, Paris would have been worse, so I guess this is the best I can do for now. Are you going to tell me that was one week? Jesus Zachy. A

To: Aline M
Sender: Zaccheus W

>Odd being back, without you and Russia. If you look in your little black book you'll find I took the liberty of putting in my address. See Z, last, least. If the handwriting offends cut it off. It was out on the phone table, I didn't sneak it out of your bag, but mea maxima culpa. They make little hand-made paper address books here; can I send you one to make amends? Glad to have you quit Paris for New York, now you only need to quit New York for Chillicothe and the paint will flow, no? Weren't you saying He abolished distance? Right beside you, Z

That was then, this is now.

Now she knows, three months on, distance is real and NASA lies. Does she detect, after ninety mails, a drop in temperature? That ancient cellular certainty, infallible as the tiny flared receptors in the walls of a waiting seed, does something to her judgement, and along the way her nerve buds, and makes her do what she still can't believe she did. Something she can't forgive herself for but can lay ultimately at his door, ultimately, truly. Running sixty blocks won't kill it so she has to talk to him. Not on the phone – as if she could bring herself to confess, to say it out loud – and not on the Net, not after what she did. This confession must be handwritten and stuck with a stamp and posted. Then the long wait of olden mail for remission. No question of forgiveness.

So she gets up from her station, the sun setting a couple of degrees along now behind a new building, and wetfoots it back indoors in search of paper. There must be some in the whole apartment. There is, a Hermitage boxed set among the rugs in the camphorwood settle, with a matching malachite pen, so she sits down right there in the guest room and looking down on russet Central Park, begins.

Zachy,

    I have something to tell you and I don't know how to say it. It's not what you think – that you know. This is something I can't believe I did, but it can't be undone. You have to forgive me, Zachy, you just have to or I don't know what I'll do, how I'll live with myself. You know how you felt when you snuck your name into my address book and wanted to make amends? Well multiply that by a billion, by a billion googols, and you'll not begin to know how I feel. I tried many times in the last few mails to tell you, I really tried, but I couldn't get it out. Yesterday I almost said it in the second mail, the one you hung on, remember, and then my courage failed me. That's why I brought up the topic of getting info on you off the Net, but I choked on it. I felt sick, Zachy, physically sick. That's also why I brought up the subject of cheating a couple of days back, when I said once you start

cheating in any way it's endless. I didn't really mean in
relationships but I think you took it that way, and I let you.
I meant what I'd just done. OK, enough beating around the bush,
right? Right.

(One more quick beat: anything, Zachy, any punishment, OK?)

Here's how it happened. You remember I was going through
a paranoid phase about your mail on public computers? Well one
day I typed in your address and the first password I could think of,
just to see how secure it really was for anyone trying to get into
Zaccheus Wilding's head. Imagine my surprise when it opened
right away. You cannot. I closed it immediately, thinking I should
tell you the same day that I knew your password and it was too
easy for anyone to get in. I guess you lived with Ashwamedha all
that time as a title only you knew and then when it went public
you forgot that someone, or even everyone, or anyone, would
think of linking you with it as a sort of talisman. Anyway, I wish
to god you'd changed it, Zachy, because that night I couldn't sleep.
Just couldn't resist trying it again, only ONLY, I swear it, Zachy, to
read my own mail to you. The temptation to delete it all was
amazing, but I read it and left it be. I guess I was trying to
understand what the hell I was doing in your life. Then I saw I was
a separate folder, and there were other women in other folders.
(Really, Zachy, you could at least codename your folders.)

Well, OK, I read them.

I read them all. Like one of those epistolary novels (I never
cared for them, not enough breathing space) where you jump
from head to head. Wanting to know where I ranked, but also,
even there, to know a little more about you, where you were
coming from, though of course that was hardly the way. By that
time I had become a thief, a sort of cat burglar, because I could

sense you in the next room. There was no going back, I just went on tiptoeing through, appalled at myself. Checking on dates a bit, but not much: not a lot of overlap, I had to admit – which only made me feel worse. But you see what made me do it, don't you, Zachy? Anyway here I am, a criminal before you. I'm sorry to tell you this in such a roundabout way and add cowardice to my crime but it would have been a bit much to do it by email. And I'm very, very sorry it ever happened. I wouldn't do such a thing again but there is no way it can be undone.

Please tell me how you want to judge this. I accept your decision whatever it is. If you can find it in you to forgive me, I'd make it up in any possible way. Would it be cheeky to expect an email? Or an impertinence to end with love? A.

Pigeon post gets there too, often. Zach sits on the roof in the late September light, evenings drawing in a fraction, all those spectacular monsoon sunsets settling down at last to a milder dispensation, and reads, then rereads the letter. Gets up, walks the length of the roof and back, stands at the balustrade and looks down into the garden at the fig, trying to gauge his response, and finding to his irritation that what really irks him is not her guilt but his stupidity.

Ashwamedha. *Ashwamedha!* Ass!

The fig-tree branches beckon, the leaves flash the old signal: jump, jump. Shame, embarrassment at folly inclines him to obey; always he marvels at the disproportion of his response to things. How do other people get it right? He hunches there a long time, looking even to himself like nothing so much as one of his mother's stupefied budgies. What he liked about Aline, her plain dealing, the way she speaks as she finds, is not altered by anything in this letter. He remembers thinking as he walked the length of the concourse at the airport after waving goodbye: isn't that the best you can hope for, tenderness and good faith? She's your touchstone, lovely impossible word. With her you rehearse over and over the gap between feeling and stone.

So what does he feel now? The stone in his heart has nothing to do with this ordinary bit of snooping, which he can see from her perspective without harsh judgement, but with despair at the tyranny of distance. If she were here it would be simply resolved, but she's at the other end of the world. She's too far away to be real; he can't seriously imagine her coming here. It's not just that he has no faith in others: he has no faith in himself. Faith is the supreme presumption, and besides, wasn't he in everything unworthy? Undeserving of every girl he singled out for love. Afraid always of asking for too much, he finds no certainty except in work. The idyll in Ohio still accuses him; there he pinned the blame on himself, resolved to inhabit the present, exist in time the way music does, become sound and sounding board. In Petersburg he allowed himself to picture this new lover saving him from his demons: work, vanity, and the elder demon, despair. But the cold fact of distance between them is too great.

And yet he remembers vividly the faraway look in her eyes: there but not there right in front of him, the mystery of space resolved.

In the last remnant of light he sees his mother's large white knickers hanging like prayer flags on the rooftop washing line; another minute and the air will start to get damp. One by one he unpegs them, folding the plain heavy cotton once down the middle, and carries them down the spiral stair, the letter nestled in that soft pile.

RED

Aline's on her roof too, waiting. He knows it, but he doesn't know what to say, or how to say it, or when, and then it's weeks gone by and maybe already too late since it seems easiest to do something he hates himself for doing, because it's the cruellest thing, nothing. So out of impatience and guilt and pain, and uncertainty and loss, but also light and failing light, is fashioned love.

M *is for* M ouse

See also M andalay, M atisse,
      M arguerite

M ouse

The optical mouse glows red. Touch it ever so lightly and it brightens like a brakelight, then dims back down until you shift it again. Fine mechanisms (a laser beam guides it) need protection so I find it a cover. Its new home is embroidered with orange and yellow nasturtiums: after forty years my mother's teacosy finds a use. There is a pigeonhole, now a mousehole, in this old mapmaker's desk that could have been made to order. The mouse lives in there snug in its cosy. Mouse cosy.

Here is a mystery. The very day the mouse is hooked up the house is invaded by mice. A modern house with no history of mice. I even find one on this desk in the pigeonhole where the speakers sit. So there are now two mouseholes, the optical mouse mousehole and the real mouse mousehole. At night the sound of a mouse nibbling, on paper, on plastic, can fill a room. Every time I turn the light on the mouse goes quiet; to zero in on it I need to switch off the light. I sit here in the dark by the light of the speakers – a stellar blue – waiting for the nibbling to start. It's tempting to lunge with a ruler when I think I'm oriented but I don't. I'm afraid I'll damage the flat screen. I need a mousetrap.

I go to the hardware man in Dharampur and he says go to a

pots and pans man. The pots and pans man says go to the Pearl Market. I go past the jeweller at the Y in Paltan Bazaar, take the right road past the rank fowl market and the fish market and the tarpaulin surdy and the paper-bag makers and the artichoke-leaf-fritter seller. Mousetraps must be getting close. But I lose my way in a lane of rope merchants and come out in a little square of school-uniform tailors. Go back to Machine Tool Alley, the rewritable CD man explains, go past the blind man with the rat poison and pyjama drawstrings, and ask at the corner shop with the watering cans what the shooting-stick maker's hours are. But I don't want a shooting-stick, I explain. He casts a long-suffering look at me from between the gel pens and PassPass packets; daily he must suffer cretins. He makes mousetraps on the *side*, he says. But I get hopelessly lost and go home empty-handed. Then, obligingly, the real mouse withdraws. Perhaps the cat got it, or the pale harrier.

I sit here stroking the optical mouse, this pet of the future that will soon give the cat its comeuppance. Every day I pull it out by the tail: it lights up high red instantly. Its joy infects me.

And then just when it has taken my heart, it sinks its teeth into my finger.

Mouse-click syndrome. At the knuckle where the index finger meets the metacarpals a heat has been gathering over the past weeks, a heat that remains after the source is switched off, as if the flesh were cooking. Man hock, microwaved hand. As if a grain of kryptonite were lodged in the knuckle, releasing its malign and terminal bale. In time what was heat begins to look like pain. Every few seconds a shower of electrons streams into the cartilage and bombards helpless tissue. A pain as hot as balm: pain and relief share the same features. At first I thought I might have knocked my knuckle, a gardening accident. I switched hands, trained the left and laggardly side, and sure enough the pain transferred to the knuckle of the left hand. I trained the outer fingers to click and yes, the heat tracked on down.

So now I know. No gardening accident, no green kryptonite: this pain is red. Optical mouse red.

Do I believe in omens?

She arrives the very day I confirm the diagnosis. I meant to run a quick search with the keywords optical mouse+pain+injury+ergonomic+maybe red, but I'm late so I simply jump into the old Fiat and drive to Delhi to meet her flight.

M andalay

Age fourteen, mother Hispanic American, father Anglo-Indian. Skin milk coffee, hair black, wiry, wild, her mother's delectably unbuttoned lower lip, her father's unfortunate ears which the hair successfully hides. I spot her at once. A skeleton! She breezes past customs and pushes her trolley along the ramp like a seasoned catwalker. My hands are shaking, my mouth dry. I can tell she's nervous too because she's got sunglasses on, bad strategy when you are expecting to be recognized by a stranger, which to all accounts I am. But I have her name on a placard, in large letters, in red, and place myself squarely in her line of vision. It's not true about American schools: she can read. She waves and shouts and gives the trolley a great push so I collect it on my shins and pain and pleasure unite seamlessly. Olivia's daughter.

Fourteen! That exquisite year at the end of the second semester of life. Every seven years the body replaces itself, she tells me in one of her letters, every last cell renewed so there's nothing that was there before. What is it that persists, she wants to know, confident I have the answer to all metaphysical questions. I who have ended the seventh semester, who feel the first breath of autumn, would be happy for an answer. I look at her now, motile perfection, every system sound on her last day of spring.

She arrives, her stock of pretzels already diminished, and I bundle her straight into the car meaning to find the shortest way out of town (*see* D elhi) to National Highway 58, north. But she needs, she insists, to be clothed, and she has found the place on the Net.

'I can't arrive *naked*, Papadumb,' She looks down at her navy blue bellbottom jeans bleached in a leg-like swathe down the front and back so the wearer looks X-rayed. See-through was my first impression back in the airport concourse, and then the mouse T-shirt, black, with Minnie's white ears strategically placed. But it pleases me that she thinks of arriving as something still to come, in Dariya Dun, not Delhi. 'They're just off Outer Ring Road near the Asian Games Village.'

This from a girl twenty seconds into India; I peel meekly off the Dhaulakuan roundabout. It turns out she's been on the phone to the shop. And sure enough they have four bespoke shalwar kameez suits ready. We leave Richie's of Shahpurjat with her in the first set, a pure white crêpe suit with a white seersucker dupatta thrown over her shoulders. Olivia's daughter.

It's three hours later, at the halfway stop, that the accident happens.

We're walking back to the car in the parking lot of the Cheetal Grand where we stopped for cheese pakodas and cold coffee when I notice the red stain.

'Hey, you sat down on the ketchup.'

She knows straight off, keeps walking till we reach the car, then sits down in the passenger seat and bursts into tears. It's started. The excitement, the strain, the fatigue brought it on. And even as I sit there comforting her and twiddling the ignition key and racking my brains for the next move, I recall a hot afternoon when *I* was fourteen. It's the middle of June, mid-siesta, the small-town streets empty, and I've been sent out on my bicycle into the afternoon to find a chemist who stocks sanitary towels. Mother or sister, I can't tell which, has been caught short, and I ride across a wide uneasy Rubicon with a strange heat in my heart that has nothing to do with the fierce sun. Monthlies.

Now I must repeat the feat. But, no: she will not let me leave the car, not for a moment. She insists on conversing as if nothing has happened (or is happening to the seat below her), talking about how nice it is not to be looked at, here. We get home three hours later, the incident weighing vaguely on us. The house looks ordinary; all my window dressing in vain. M disappears to the bathroom, I hear the crackle of the old shower cap, idle since O's departure.

She reappears in the magenta and black suit. Subdued, but determined to be impressed: she remarks on little things she remembers, big things that have changed. The white suit is soaking in a basin of bleach. Next morning I find a row of little black flags on the washline: she's cut up the mouse T-shirt. Towels. Olivia's daughter.

I want to kiss those rags.

I phone for a home-delivery lunch. When Garg comes to the door I'm in the shower. Flurried, I take the delivery with one hand as I fumble with the other among monsoon damp notes in my wallet; in the confusion an extra note passes between us. Both of us spot the mistake together but he closes his fist on the cash and asks politely for a glass of water while folding the uncounted notes into his shirt pocket to spare himself the dilemma of counting them. I fetch him the water, wait while he drinks and thank him, disappointed less in him than in myself for being unable to speak up. Such a small note, a tenth of the price of the lunch – I could consider it a tip – a thousandth of the cost of yesterday's garment shopping – but it spoils the lunch. I mellow too late: my sudden change of mood has disfigured the afternoon. M is quietly appreciative; already she's learning to make allowances for men, the first of a lifetime's series, this mature little woman.

M atisse

Apostle of red. Master of its Art. For the first time colour is allowed to be. *Is* space, extension. Distance and its nemesis. Matisse returned space to colour and colour to space.

'If you confine colour within some curved black line, say, you are ... robbing it of its expansive potential ... Once colour reaches a point that is only slightly beyond its limits, this expansive power takes effect – a kind of neutral zone comes into being where the neighbouring colour has to enter once it has reached the extent of its expansion. When that happens you could say the paint breathes.'

But then he nods off.

'What I dream of is an art which is balanced, pure and calm, devoid of any disquieting or preoccupying subject, which provides for the intellectual, the businessman, as well as for the literary artist, a soothing sedative for the brain; something like a comfortable armchair to rest from his physical tiredness.'

Oh oh. And this in 1908 at the height of his first great creative decade. If he had deliberately set out to alienate the Gertrude Steins of this world he could not have packed a more dreary hamper: *soothing, sedative, comfortable, armchair, rest*, all in one basket. Nor has he forgotten the salt. *The businessman*! What's a *businessman* doing on this picnic? The Steins would have a fit. But as ever the seed-merchant's son has his head screwed on right, while the salon ravers' are on back to front. Besides he's at this minute dealing profitably with two able Russian business-men, thanks to whom (and one revolution) the world will have access to the most comprehensive collection of Matisses under one roof.

M arguerite

I look a fright
like nothing on earth
but it could be worse
imagine the boys in black
and me in red!
(better witch than harlot)

not that I can't carry red
look at me at 14
no witch no cucking stool
just the book I'm reading and reading
(and not a word of it penetrating my skull
it could be braille under my elbow
so bored I look)
back then
but what about these guys here?
Pierre yawning over the draughtsboard
Jean debating whether to crown a king
Or chuck it with all his might into the fireplace
(all of us straining to please

RED

creeping around the house
Shh, Your Father's Working!)
Mother counting every crewel stitch
And still managing that vacant smile
(or is she really blissed out back there by herself?)
And Him with his brush held like a baton
Conducting silent music
                    And yet and yet
I must admit
he's given me space in this windowless room
set me free as a sprite given me green clogs a book
a look that says I've just had news the world
could be my oyster only I'm condemned first
to dwell in brackets between the shells
wade in that warm expensive phlegm
for youth's eternity
no pearl in sight
unless it's black
                (me)

N *is for* N arrator

Also N ag, N agina, N agouri

N arrator

Me, N.

Halfway between A and Z. Well, closer by one letter to Z. (N, as friend Zaccheus reminds me, is simply Z laid on its side.)

You've met Matisse, you've met Mandalay, you've even met Matisse's daughter. Meet me.

In the middle station of life, middle class, middling build. Middle-aged too, halfway out, but also only halfway in. A foothills man, neither plainsman nor Montagnard. Like the Grand Old Duke of York who marched his men up the hill:

> *when they were up they were up*
> *and when they were down they were down*
> *and when they were only halfway up*
> *they were neither up nor down.*

Nice view from there: not high, not low. Middle-falutin. I have a middle initial too, E, recall, but that's neither here nor there. The ears I've mentioned. Nose a small portable hatchet, throat parched outside but not in, bathroom singer. Jawline tense from facing the world alone, latterly. Slight shadow on the chin since I usually can't be bothered shaving till late in the day (too late?); hair steel shavings. Eyebrows on the credit side: O was always running a finger along them as if tracing their fine wide sweep for the ultimate mannequin; eyes debit, since one is more brown than blue and one more blue than brown. Would-be painter's fingers. Weakness for blue, O's favourite colour too.

But sucker for red.

N: a sweet midpoint from where you see the whole book spread out like a patchwork quilt from your lost nursery, each square an alphabet with its picture, your first glimpse of the idea of a series.

Halfway in, but work's piling up. I sat down here just now determined to have done with the wad of notes scribbled in the dark on the bedside table. (That hiss of graphite on paper, that middle-of-the-night stage whisper – *working!* – that finally snapped O's patience. Or was it the lead I didn't use?) Determined to plunge straight in, no shillyshallying – when a wave of hunger assailed me. Not metaphysical hunger, not aesthetic, not spiritual need, not even lust. Simple hunger. Food. So I fried up a batch of pappadams, dreaming all along of O's Oaxacan roast eggplant with green peppers and toasted black sesame seed. Stewed figs with Kahlua on creamed rice for afters. With or without a garnish of banana flowers, ancient fertility symbol but also (see K angra) when the stalk is half formed, dildo.

Hunger – now to the power of two. We forage in the doolie, my mother's venerable meatsafe, scour the fridge. I make a sandwich for Manda, who was hoping for shahi mutton with tandoori rotis. For me a smorgasbord of intangibles. Greed as I dream of her mother's cooking. Lust as I dream of her mother. Tiredness from overdoing the houseclean. Depression, as old as this clay. Embarrassment, from yesterday when I made an ass of myself at the jeweller's. Annoyance from ten minutes ago when M dropped a slab of foreign chocolate in the sink. I rinsed it and rinsed it because it's too precious to throw away, here. Doesn't she understand? (How could she?) But also satisfaction, ten seconds old, at the rescuing of this event, still too fresh to count as memory, for use in the book. So finally life and art meet.

Life rules.

Here's a fact: Matisse was born the same year as Gandhi, 1869, but outlived him by five years. Painters live longer, look around. Poets die young, romantic poets, novelists in middle age (*see* H eart). So it's easy to panic, throw out all those scribbled notes. Skip meals (every missed meal sends the blood-fat levels soaring, and it's clots that kill, not cholesterol), lose your red pencil, bash straight through to the final draft.

But the truth is it's the first draft that's the truth. That mass of tangled pencillings with a blank half circle where the lamp base sits as paperweight on the bedside table, all those under-written overwritings in the dark, indecipherable in the morning. Except your editor will not accept raw material, will you, Sam? Eyes closed is still the best draft, but double spaced is the rule. Prose is like squid, the longer you cook the tougher it gets. Raw is tough too, besides it's not cuisine and could hurt you. Ten seconds in hot oil, then a twist of lemon and asparagus, lightly steamed. Heaven. O showed me. With life it's the opposite. Life is shin meat: long simmering is best.

Life rules, even while it rules itself out. Example. Last month I should have been writing my book but when I sat down at this desk Manda's letter with its neat round writing, her current choice out of the great welter of scripts that await her unformed hand, lay there accusingly. It had been staring at me for three days.

I really had meant to reply straight away. So I dialled up the server, rapped the table impatiently while the alien was strangled. *Scrawgascreegascrewgascraygascrum*. Through.

To: Mandalay
From: Pa

>JUST *as I sat down to work I saw your letter and I knew if I didn't get the reply off today, the weekend would be here and then the mason would have his foot in the door, and workaday stuff would take over. So I have a proposition. Is it OK if I write to you and write the book at the same time? Write these letters into the book?*

Comes the reply:

To: Me
From: Mandalay

>Poppa*dumb, NO!*

End of notion. No more Mandamail.

So you smuggle her into a subplot, half afraid that life will take some terrible revenge. Do I know enough about her now? When her childhood lay all around me I was tied up with other books. The few pages of close observation, a birdwatcher's loving notes, came to nothing. Now both of us have travelled on. Where is that man? Where has that girl gone? This one's here, aged fourteen, dancing in the next room (thud, smack, thud go her bare feet on the cement floor) right when I have a deadline.

Wasn't it the same with Olivia? Life dumbing down inspiration because it knows there's no contest. Neglect her at your peril, attend to her and you're lost. Is the marriage contract at fault? Marriage makes a career out of love, the way writing makes a career out of inspiration. The habit of love, old love become custody. The imagery is telling: the other night, after years of absence, O appeared in a dream, so real I'm sure I sat up in bed. In the dream I saw myself walking beside someone to the end of a yard where there was to be an exchange of hostages. The one beside me was to be exchanged for the other waiting there. But when we got there this one turned around and faced me: *Olivia!* She'd been with me all along. There was no need for an exchange, her arm said, locking with mine. It was the other who was a fraud. *Her* face I couldn't see at all, but her body looked young.

Do you meet the same woman again and again or different women in the same guise? Do you write the same book over and over? The habit of love, the habit of scribbling. I'm back to sleeping at the muezzin's wake-up call: a.m. and p.m. divide my day again: ante mullah, post mullah. I wake four hours later, tired: I wake up wide awake like a ham actor; lie there writing on the backs of old drafts before washing the gum from my eyes. All later writing is secondary. Can I forget?

4 am–5:15 am, the day she left. I have the pages. Yellowing relics, proof: the jottings that finally sent her away. I remember lying awake in the dark, eyes closed for fear of losing those waking thoughts, that clear wet dictation that goes on and on. O turns over every time the baby cries next door, a train whistles. Muezzin 1 is overtaken by muezzin 2 from a nearer mosque, the better voice erased. She has pulled the sheet over her face, a light sleeper who hates streetlights, dripping taps, frogs, cicadas, screech owls, the brainfever bird, scribbling pencils. An hour and fifteen minutes I scribble, on and off, eyes closed, gold in those tailings, till I decide it's too late to go to sleep again so I might as well get up. She lies there, a sheeted corpse, murder in her heart. I take the pages to my study to unravel. And find them blank!

God's truth. His joke. The pencil lead was broken (I have the pencil too). The pages bore the imprint of a wooden point, line after line of faint indecipherable passion.

Nothing drove her away, a surplus of nothing.

Z is my comfort: he makes this isolation supportable. *He'll* make something of his life. But I keep him clear of Manda. The day after he got back from Russia we met at Barista.

Z: Old stick in the mud! [*Why weren't you there?*]

N: Rootless cosmopolitan! [*Nice to have you back!*]

Z: Pig of a bourgeois! [*Showing me up, right?*]

N: Gipsy! [*If I could afford to skip off I would.*]

Z: Homemaker! [*I may just have found someone to replace my mother.*]

N: What was Matisse, then? [*Marry her, idiot, not your muse.*]

Do we ever say what we mean? Do we ever mean what we say? Don't fritter your life away in work, I want to tell him. Just live. Grab her with both hands. But I see him going my way, hell bent on becoming me.

Right now I want to sound him out on a vital point, but he prevaricates, pretends another concern.

Z: [*Earnest, leaning towards me, the acolyte.*] Is it hard being better than better-known guys?

N: No, it's easy. So, how was she? Did the earth move?

Z: [*Eyes going molten.*] No.

N: *No!*

Z: No, the sky just cracked open and the universe bent back on itself and light boiled over and God opened one eye.

N: Oh, OK.

So I was not surprised when the olive tree arrived. Not branch, *tree*.

N ag the king cobra, *Naja bungaris*

N agina the female of the species *Naja bungaris*, deadlier than the male. The Doms believe that if you kill Nag you must kill Nagina too. When Nag is killed the killer's image is imprinted on the dead one's eye. The spouse studies this image and comes looking for you.

N agouri goddess of the blackshorts, wife and protectress of the current leader [see *Annals of the Black Codpiece Society*, by E. Trotter, evidently a unicum]: she has no identifiable ancestry in any classified faith, the ordinary practice of grafting a woman's head onto a snake's body being here reversed.*

> *Reader here is a ladder strait to* **O**
> *Shun you the pit of snakes that yawns below*

---

* In 2002 a Japanese doctoral student travelling in the Shivalik hills above Rishikesh was offered an illustrated manuscript, which she promptly bought. The so-called *Nagatarangini*, an unbound collection of eight numbered folios now lodged in Kobe University, caused a stir in art-historical circles for this was the earliest example of Nagouri painting on paper. While the subject of snake worship is not an uncommon one among painters throughout the land, the worship of the hamadryad (the king cobra, *Naja bungaris*) in its feminine or Nagina form associated with the Devi or mother goddess is. Preliminary studies, by no means conclusive, suggest a link with an immeasurably older tradition of representing and worshipping the Devi in her Nagina theophany, a tradition that has its roots in the very hills where the manuscript surfaced. The great Shiva, who wears a serpent necktie, is a montane god (his consort is Parvati, 'of the hills', and their daughter, the Ganges, has a Himalayan source), but Shiva is himself a late entrant and a sentimentalization of one strand in a robust pre-Hindu animism whose many and curious evidences strew the country and stretch back some fifty thousand years. In other schools of Indian painting Shiva is sometimes shown, either alone or in conjunction with the other two members of the Vedic trinity, Brahma and Vishnu, adoring the Devi or mother goddess, but until the *Nagatarangini* appeared he had never as far as scholars can determine

RED

been represented as her literal follower. His depiction in these eight folios (to judge by his customary properties of trident and leopardskin, or sometimes tigerskin, to say nothing of the cobra necktie (although D. P. Kainthola has argued in the *Journal of Aryan Philology* that the necktie may be a common or garden wattle)), as following her lead, the second in a group of five men following the Devi, suggests a chronological posteriority whose implications in the light of his subsequent usurpation are one of history's rich ironies.

The traces of the mass extermination of snake-worshippers by sun-worshippers, references to which occur in the Hindu epics and late Vedic literature, are fragmentary and presumptive, but the process likely lasted centuries. The *Nagatarangini* is a defiant and at the same time innocent evocation of an earlier state; by eliding all reference to the holocaust in the subcontinent and merely showing a procession of deities and humans it quietly, and perhaps even inadvertently, makes a point. Its iconography bears striking morphological congruities with both the prehistoric Dhulia cave paintings in the valley of the Alaknanda, tributary of the Ganges, and with a later popular tradition of niche painting whose itinerant artists, very often musicians as well as painters, were active as late as the twentieth century, perhaps even up to the present. For example, in the niche paintings of certain seventeenth- and eighteenth-century houses in the Shivalik region we find a woman with a cobra head leading a group of men, always five in number. The procession in the *Nagatarangini* bears a striking resemblance to the drawings of caves II A and B at Dhulia, destroyed in the earthquake of 1991, while also precisely foreshadowing the work of popular muralists centuries later. We must either pretend that a single painter visited the caves in question and then travelled the length and breadth of the region painting the same scene, or assume the existence of a popular tradition of painting descending from antiquity, all the more astonishing for having survived in cults among the descendants of the defeated to the present day. The recurrence of this particular motif of the Nagouri procession in contemporary truck and autorickshaw paintings testifies to the resilience of what may be the oldest continuous painting tradition in the world. The significance of the last figure in the row of followers, commonly represented as a crested lizard-headed creature, is not known.

— V. Agnihotri, J. Cline, K. O'Boyle, S. Banerji, and E. Sasaki, eds., *The Nagatarangini, a facsimile edition*, Kobe, 2004.

Were you not warned, good reader? Now turn tail
Take no medal and go you strait to **Jail**

O *is for* O live

See also O ctober, O dalisque,
O=nothing

O live

She runs a Google search, *olive trees+mature+delivered*, orders, pays, a Spanish company from Barcelona. A local bylaw, the man explains, enunciating the foreign language, prohibits the export of trees older than a hundred years. Also, certain American states prohibit the importation of European trees unless they're pollen-less cultivars. Air-pollution laws. It's not for America, she says. Can you deliver to India? A moment's silence. India. Why not?

And one mature, root-boxed olive, *Leccino* cultivar, crated, boards a DHL flight to Delhi. She tracks its passage and arrives herself the day after. Follows it by road – eyes shut against the driving – in the Thomas Cook car, thank god for air conditioning, and astonishes Zach at his door.

Mrs Wilding won't have it. Zach could have told Aline that but she took him by surprise. Won't have the olive and won't have an American dowager, her word, to Zach, when Aline is safely lodged in the best hotel. She looks appraisingly at her son: what *does* he get up to on these foreign jaunts? Her burnt-caramel forehead crimps at the memory of his conception. His duteous father, hockey Olympian, dead these thirty years.

Zach is looking at Aline: now what's unreal about her is that she's here. She's bejaysus *here*! He keeps touching her as if to make sure. She returns the look, her red nails stroke his back, his sides, amusement rounding out her love: will nothing satisfy this man? In fact something will, only he's afraid to speak it out loud. He has this mad notion of throwing up his music-teacher job and laying out an olive grove, a farm where they dig and delve together, but can't bring himself to speak, much less to hope. It's a wet valley, better suited to pianos than olives.

And so the tree sits out by the gate in its box, the lid off, subject of the locals' curiosity. SORRY, ZACHY! painted, in red, on the crate. Stray dogs sniff at the planks, picking up foreign smells and pollens, lift their legs at one corner and trot off satisfied. Cats are more wary, more persistent; a dove is already contemplating one branch near the top.

O ctober

No month as fine as this. The heat gone, cold not yet come. Air still moist from the long rains, afternoon light so mellow it brings tears to the eye. Storms of butterflies; woodsmoke from the first brush fires; every sense rejoicing. Fresh breezes up on the roof at night under a harvest moon. At the end of a hard day, every muscle reporting on the dig around the avocado stump, you find the corners of your mouth stretch into an unbidden smile. You throw your head back and send a silent shout into the sky. *Yes!*

Time passes.

Your breathing lengthens, levels out, grows quieter. Close your eyes and listen, focus where the nostrils meet the upper lip. On and on goes the even flow of breath: it could be flowing either way, it's hard to tell. It's as if the adult past were cancelled and you had discovered again the child's way of dwelling without strife in a continuous present. Take your pulse. It's all over the place, lunatic ramblings, and yet you feel immune. The sheltering spirit informs this branch, that stone, the suddenly opening passage of bright air that says: this way. Not even childhood gave this sense of entering into things. You touch objects lightly, they touch you back. A sense of being supported, even of floating. You are mortal, you are content. You are dying, you are happy.

Your daughter is asleep in the house below.

Rapture of this order should alert one: *Devil: Next Crossing*. At the very least irony might signpost *Steep Descent*. But irony, the word, the idea, like Devil, sounds antique, profitless. The world is still killing – on the Zee*bytes* home page a jumpy soldier confronts the camera – and yet the feeling persists. At any moment the phlebitis in your calf can release the fatal clot – but not yet, not this month.

The moon shines and the drumstick leaves shiver and here already is November with its uncertainties: the shawl that ends up being simply carried, the bedside window left carelessly open. *Vainglory*, calls the hawk cuckoo over the grave of summer, *vainglory!* Going to lock the gate you walk into a spider's web slung clear across the lawn by luck and daring. Back out of it cautiously and find the rigging, line and curve and bracket, imprinted on your lenses. Spider lurking on the frame.

Where do we go when our transports let us down? N, confirmed pen-and-ink man, goes down and writes these two rapid pages straight onto the screen. *Care, Devil: Man at Work.*

At the muezzin's call I shut down, look in at Manda's room and spread a rug over her feet where she can reach down and pull it up.

O dalisque

Wednesday Zach misses coffee at Barista. A whole week since Aline arrived but he's kept her well hidden. What's he afraid of? Me?

Then they turn up together.

Z rattles the gate latch and walks in. A stands there, framed by the squared-off brick arch. *Odalisque in red trousers*. Matisse had a model in Nice with the same mix of weariness and tigress sensuality. This one is dressed but you can see where the breasts make theory of rayon; the cloven leaves of my mountain ebony wrap her about like Eve in the garden. The shattering beauty Z's been bragging about I'm not so sure of; I have a harder, less susceptible eye. Besides, she's my age, so I can see the defects, know where to look. In good tilth, though. Young Zach doesn't understand there's no mystery to flesh: it's simply firm one minute and starting to sag the next. Besides, in his besotted haze he sees the whole, and then just the glow of the whole, not the details; I can see by the way he's looking at her, he was afraid to introduce us sooner. I can see also she wants to meet this prodigy called N: Zach has been boasting about me (the mutual-admiration society chugs on).

They come on a day when Manda and I are wondering what to do about lunch (last night I saw her stiffen at the dread clatter of blackeye peas at the bottom of a pan, and poured them straight back into the jar unsoaked). Not one but two Americans gathered under this roof, so naturally I order pizza. Both protest the decision but I'm doing this for me.

Zach looks harassed, overworked. I can see he's stretched to breaking trying to juggle A and his mother and his job. He explains, aside, about the tree, invokes our history: no request can be turned down, right, please, no, yes? I look at him. Is he mad? Doesn't the ass twig I *want* an olive? Ninety-nine years old, no less, on a plate. I think back to a night under the stars in a Greek olive grove. Yes, I'll take it, Zach. There's no room for it in the yard, more's the pity. But it can go outside, where the avocado fell in the storm. A bit boggy there but I can build a special bed for it, to separate it from the willow, which actually likes its feet wet.

Aline is delighted when I accept. I play the dove, peacemaker, pretend I'm obliging her. The fact is I'm stricken, as every man she ever meets must be, or must have been. She sees, is pleased, but in a detached way, scoring some forgotten point. But I get no encouragement, no lift, as we used to say. No drag, but. I show her the garden, naming local names, English, Latin, the ones I know. She takes up a fallen coral flower and looks into its crimson depths.

'It seems almost a pity to give them names.'

The reproach is gentle enough but I'm stung into justification.

'Olive is a name.'

'True.'

No scholastic sparring, no logic chopped. Her touch on my arm is strangely thrilling.

RED

Later I examine my response and find the thrill lies precisely in that dark moment of our namelessness. I think back also of another remark, quite innocent, that nettled me. *I can see what keeps you here.* I shrugged: *It's a house.* Why did I speak loosely? I was simply annoyed that she should imagine one needed a good reason to be here. But then, could I take *her* seriously, her American life over there?

Zach brings up the story of his mother's intransigence by way of apologizing again. Aline brushes all that aside. She's taking a house next to Zach, it turns out. You can see the mumpty of her place (which she thinks will make a fine upstairs studio) from Zach's terrace. Romeo and Juliet. A year's rent up front, so the landlord's over the moon.

'Stay *here* till it's ready,' I offer, and find Manda looking at me with a child's clarity. Zach looks surprised too. What am I up to?

I confess I'm bowled over: A seems to me to be carrying a burden, easily enough, but looking for a suitable waystation; while I, in constant danger of floating away, seem in need of ballast. It seems only right that we should meet in this alphabet of chance. After all, **A** is forever condemned to go in search while **Z** simply waits, godlike, half deaf (except to his own music). What if **N** were to stick out his foot as she goes by?

But she's immune, like Manda: your creation is always impervious to your charms. She smiles at my offer, nods a nod that encompasses a world of replies, and follows Zach down the Venturi side of the house. He wants to show off the brick folly.

I pause a moment to imagine the olive's new home. I can see it domiciled already, fruiting under another sun, leaning a little, the way I like, after many harvests. (Why am I standing there alone?) It's in a brick hold, the mossed bricks laid crosswise on their sides, to raise the boxed earth six inches above the surrounding ground. This past monsoon it shed its leaves and had me worried but it has begun to leaf again, grey-green buds pushing out of the bare branch, like new horns on a calf. The old leather shoe I left at the roots, the way Moroccans do, is decaying nicely. It's a winter afternoon, sunlight sloping under a bank of violet cloud. I go back in the gate she stood at years ago, framed there, and sit on the harp seat. The stone head of my rock totem is lit down one side to the promontory of the chin. The light looks kindly (I know it's not). And I continue my old interrogation, talking out loud, but softly, to ghosts. You. You. And you, are *you* fading too, of all people? I gave you my whole heart, held nothing back, as never before. My breath was mortgaged to you. But even hearts can fail you. Listen to it now, on a five per cent ration. A passage about the diameter of this spidersilk feeds it blood.

I sit there unaware of the chalk line being scrawled on my gate by a gipsy-looking man. Then I shuffle indoors for tea. Slip into the old dateless haze, no paper, no TV, just raptures and happenchance. In the kitchen I let fate pick the menu. Does my little finger brush against the fork as I reach for the knife? I will use a fork to cut with. I have led my life and now I'm following. Just when I think *fruit* my eye rests on a pear. I pick it up, eat it. I stand at the window and watch a pair of nesting sevensisters pecking to shreds the hemp rope that ties the bamboo trellis. It's time it was dismantled anyway. Shall I go up on the roof and call on Her in the oratory, the miniature Coptic Virgin I stole as a young man in Luxor? I look up: *shock* of morning glory! Heavenly blue, a pledge. Saying: spare yourself the climb, I'm here. You live for such moments. Well, no, you live and the moments come.

Pizza wakes me. The delivery boy at the gate looks familiar

when he takes off his spaceman helmet. Eyes of different colours and says his name's Trotter. If you had told me ten years ago you could get pizza delivered in this town I'd have had you certified.

Manda falls to in spite of herself, Zach is not far behind. Aline nibbles out of politeness, picking out the green ring of an olive to look through. I watch my family greedily. If I could only paint.

O = zooks, nothing

When they're gone I check first the postbox, no letters, then the mail. A reply to my mail of last week entitled *O live here! Olivia*:

> N
>
> >*Things are looking up for a change* [she's met somebody].
> *Couple of new clients. Went to see* Carmen *last night* [with
> him, and also: When did you last see *Carmen* in DD?] *Dinner
> in a little Afghan tent that just came up.* [We can get your
> stuff too] *Don't know if it's wise to go away just now. Let me
> think about this.*
>
> O

I think about it too. Is my wheedling undignified? Don't I already regret the loss of silence? Am I better off with my painted Virgin and the ink flowing freely? I put her in a pumpkin shell and there I keep her very well.

And yet, if O came back I would be her silence and she would be my speech. And if her presence killed a book wouldn't the trees rejoice?

A gust shakes the copse I've planted and the trees nod their heads.

P *is for* P ole

See also P ayal, P rivacy, P aintbox

P ole

This time he'll go alone. Trust no one: simpler that way. No one pulls you up, no one lets you down.

Gilgitan sets down his basket of bitter gourd, this model prisoner, and looks around. Exhibition day and he mans the vegetable stall. The jail walls are fifty feet away. Right now there's nobody in the way but it's the middle of the day. He's never trusted daylight with its nothing-new face. He turns the basket so the fattest greenest gourds face forward: presentation, now there's something he's learnt in here. Picks up by the tail a fallen gourd, twirls it, and slots it back into place nose first, an errant mouse.

In the next basket along a white eggplant sits among the purple like a cuckoo's egg. A sport, its swirl of throwback freckles catches the one o'clock sunlight and spins it back out to infinity.

By the second day of the show the cabbage skirts have begun to fray at the hem. The lettuces are done for but the tomatoes have just begun to hug their hot young dream of never-ending red. By day three, today, all the produce has lost its shine, exhausted from repeated sprinkling. But attendance is up, it's Sunday, and the townspeople file past the giant force-fed marrows, idle prodders and handlers and bruisers who ignore every notice in the two languages they can read.

Again no one looking. G crams a whole tomato in his mouth – just when the warden appears from nowhere. So he springs to attention, juicing it with just his cheek muscles, teeth clenched like it's not there, his jaw a vice, his tongue pushing up against the palate with all his might like he's kissing the pig girl (what's she up to?) at attention, arms rigid, eyes bulging, furious impassive crushing. The way a lizard goes when it's gobbling up something wider than its head and suddenly a rival appears.

'Last day, Gilgitan,' the warden nods at the stalls. Goes to snap a green bean but finds it bends about his fingers.

'Shar,' Gilgitan gets out, with, miracle, no juice.

Suddenly he realizes why he has to go, why he can't serve his term and let them let him go. Because they've made a mouse of him. They almost made him theirs, especially this duff dickshit of a warden he's learnt to sir.

Anyway, to back out now would be truly mousy after all the groundwork. Yesterday he unhooked the tallest bamboo in the marquee and laid it under the last of the long trestle tables with the display baskets. It was one of the middle poles so it was not likely to be missed; the tent top simply sagged at that point and since no one had seen a cloud for weeks it was not likely to fill with rain and leave a telltale drip. All he had to do was wait till the warden turned his back and then grasp and lift the pole out of its makeshift tenthole.

And make a hole too, for the top end to go in, but that he's done during the past month over at the foot of the wall, an inch a day, half an inch, some days no more than the dirt under his fingernails. It looks like a snakehole but it musn't be bottomless.

When it was the right depth he plugged it with a stone, then tamped the stone in, then day by day widened the mouth. He can't afford to miss. The pole must go in first time; no second chance.

This evening. It must be light enough for him to see, dark enough not to be seen.

Mother of all snakes, wife of the cohorts, help me.

The pole has an iron cap with a spike in it that fits into a eyelet in the tentcloth. Now it must find another hole. He'll use it for sighting, that tip. That's the top of the bamboo, the narrow flexible end he'll use for the vault. The other end, heavy, rough, weathered, will bear him up, and over.

Aim it like a spear. Hold it like a lover.

Pulling out the pole was nothing. He's still young. The splinter in his thumb is nothing. It looks like a bee sting, he thinks and glances again at the wall. His hands were always hard; jail digging made no difference.

Last night he lay with his hands folded under his head, listening for the last time to the flying foxes in the fig tree outside the barred window. Head-down creatures feeding in the cool night air, feeding and moving on. Lay listening to the leathery rattle of leaves at each small tug, heard the tick as the fig parted company with the stem and passed into the soft black mouth. Imagined a delicate set of claws opening, releasing the branch – saw the body swing out of true, then swing back as the small slack fist sought a hold at the next cluster of fruit. That is the action he loves, that moment of letting go, when your hands leave the pole and you hang there suspended between horizontal and vertical, after you have climbed as far as you can, before you begin to come down. If one could just hang there forever.

He has the pole in his hands, but the light is wrong. The sun is in his eyes and it should be behind the other wall, behind him. The warden is shouting something as he moves towards him. He must go now but he can't see the hole. Someone has filled it in but he must go now, now. He starts his run, levels the pole aims it at a point just short of the wall and digs in. He's borne up, up, as the pole bends, but there's not enough give in the wood and he hasn't gained enough height and he goes smack into the wall and falls back into the jail yard. That was last night's dream.

Now the light is right. The last tables have been cleared and the best produce is on its way to the senior officers' bungalows. Nobody looking. Go, boy.

He levels the pole, sights with the tip, breathes in, and runs.

Digs in. Hole!

Hup.

He's flying.

P ayal Silver chain worn on ankle.

Not funny is her new mantra. She's on that precarious edge (have I not already sensed this in her letters?): tiring of childish things, and straightaway lapsing back into them. Sick, for example, of my silly jokes but still enamoured of them. So: *Not funny*, no exclamation mark, with an adult sneer held for four seconds till she bursts out laughing. I dread the drying up of that spring; it's what waters our fragile garden. Long after I'm sick myself of her giggling, closeted in her room with her new friend, Richa from next door, I inflict the jokes, relentlessly, my heart in my mouth, like some incorrigible magician flicking out ever gaudier silk scarves.

Is she a nuisance, already? Right in the middle of a line she slips into the study to borrow the glue stick: doesn't clomp – she's too subtle for that – but it's like the old days. The whole house is hers but just when I'm poised to write she needs this corner. Or she's pounding away in her own room at the old typewriter, every key resounding through the house – how did we manage in the old days? – a punch in the head. The laptop is too much like home and she can't possibly do anything so childish as write by hand.

Already I grudge her her moods, her nerves. It's not like Aline's problem, or Marguerite's: life in Daddy's shadow. My Manda

221

doesn't have *that* worry. But still, measuring up to expectations must have its trials and tensions. Ease off, I want to tell her (but don't), you don't have to be the best. But it's clear she has to be: all she needs is to find out what in. My unspoken lecture resounds between her Walkmanned ears, set to Bollywood's thieveries.

For now she has a solution. Everything must be Indian.

From day one and the white crêpe shalwar kameez that came to grief at the Cheetal Grand – she has set about refitting herself as if for life's new semester.

My fault for feeding the flames with clippings of Ash and Bipash and all the Bollywood Khans, but her mother has already laid the kindling with her yOGa and her Odissi dance and her militant vegetarianism. School balanced the scales over there, and New York was ready ballast, but freed of America she veers right around and is born again.

Language is where it all breaks down, naturally. She speaks no more than a dozen words of Hindi. But that only makes her the more determined: everything *else* must be right.

'I just *love* Indian.'

Our hosts at dinner look puzzled at several apparent lapses, grammar the least. She means the food, and is helping herself generously, a growing child, to the kidney beans; India is a flavour where she comes from, an indulgence. She's clever enough to see her mistake, but the sudden access of attention is oddly gratifying in the midst of her welcome new-found invisibility. Accustomed to being indulged for her difference over there, she can't tell what it is she's missing; she craves both specialness and invisibility. The next time she specifies 'Indian sweets', but even that mystifies her new friend: what other kind of sweet is there?

Richa is a teenager in awe of her TV accent. When she gives

RED

Manda a set of payals as a troth of eternal friendship it's less a pledge to the future than the severing of a last tie with their childish past. She slips them on her friend's slender feet (Olivia's feet, her one vanity, forgiven in a dancer) and Manda will not be parted from them. I hear her cross the cool terrazzo tinkling as she goes, a new and adult slowness marking her passage, a heaviness not of body but of movement. Now she wants to sing Indian.

P aintbox

The range of human colour intrigues Aline.

Hill types, their skin old ivory, terracotta Tibetans who could be Chippewa, porcelain girls Alexander the Great left behind, and the majority a dark mass in every earth hue from ochre to coal black. Then what they wear. She must get it down, soon. For now she stands at the gate, a monstrous slice of wedding cake with a sewing-machine wheel at the latch, and peers at the world.

Night birdcalls remind her she's not at home. And the sun comes up, pouring glair from a robin's-egg-blue sky whose varnish alone will take a tub of glycerine. Pearl-grey memories of Petersburg don't help, nor does the dim watercolour wash of Manhattan's canyons. A proper paintbox is on its way from Amazon.com, and brushes and paper; meanwhile she has the wee pocket box.

Mrs Wilding relents and sends across breakfast on a tray. Zach returns at lunchtime from the posh girls' school where he teaches; his mother taught music at Risingholme too. Their first meal together at Mrs Wilding's table was not a success, and Aline has decided to manage at home. Zach has dropped off a ten-gallon flask of mineral water that she sips, a little guardedly when she learns the tamperproof seal is no guarantee it's not filled at the tap. The one thing she cannot take is the plumbing. A contractor is found who will redo both bathrooms in 72 hours, his guarantee, at a price. She'll pay, the landlord's happy.

Day one is breaking day: hammers and chisels to drive you mad. She sits on the divan with one foot up, painting her toenails. Shuts what doors she can but that's no good. Climbs the staircase to the mumpty where it's quieter and looks out at the hills.

The next day the tilers arrive: plumes of fine clay dust from their disc saws and a wailing as of PlayStation dinosaurs. They work with little balloons pulled over the fingers of the left hand, the hand that grips the tile. The tiler's assistant would like a go with the saw but is told to wait for the ivory batch; right now they're onto the expensive cherry red.

Back and forth the assistant goes, red tile cuts in his hand. The American woman is on the roof looking out at the hills. The lifting and dropping action of her head tells him she's drawing. Then he sees her painting from a little box no bigger than the palm of her hand. That's neat, very neat; that he'd like. Do a swap? Get rid of the painting for now. Ever since the cops came sniffing at the pig girl's hut he's been worried. He can always steal it back.

The American looks like some kind of movie star. Every time he goes by from the gate, where the cutting is done, he lifts his eyes to hers. She gives him a probing look. He has skin the colour of molasses, crested hair, and a saurian jaw, and he wears his tiler's balloons on his right hand.

P rivacy

So much I meant to do with her childhood and now it's gone.

I touch the curtain to widen the crack. What could she be reading about in that book? The *Family Health Manual*, held up as she lies on her back in her pyjamas, the bedside lamp on in the middle of the day. I who last summer put up a screen here to allow some privacy to two sets of house guests am violating it at the very same door. But I have a right to know how she is after last week's mysterious illness.

Last week she was sick. I cast around blindly for a children's doctor until someone pointed out she was no longer a child and I hung my head like someone caught out in a crime. I've missed her childhood was all I could think. We found a regular doctor, for grown-ups. Seeing me distraught the man said on the second visit: I didn't want to say this earlier, but these pains and numbnesses in her foot, her neck, her shoulders, could they be imagined? Is she unhappy? Is she missing home? I came back and read her copy of *Ann of Green Gables*, looking for clues. I trawled the Net, copied and pasted 'Ten things your teen won't share with you'. I even read, in the same guilty spirit of inquiry, three or four lines — no more, your honour — from her diary, and learnt the truth: she was in love. Missing her violinist. One of New York's rising stars, only fifteen. I could have wept.

This afternoon again I stand at the door of her room and watch her fall asleep reading a letter from New York. Watching over this grave handsome young woman I hardly know. She's gone to bed to sleep off a shock. A school friend, not the violinist, has died, a friend she didn't know she loved until now. Her first death. What is going through her head, love or pain? Or love and pain? Or the love of pain? I should have talked it out, but no words seemed right. When sleep comes over her, her eyelids drifting down and staying shut, it looks chillingly like death. I want to thank fate for taking that child and not this.

Should I be there at all, at that door? And these words, do they compound the crime?

Q *is for* Q uick

See also Q uid pro quo

Q uid pro quo

Next day is finishing day. The tiles are grouted with white cement and polished with a soft cloth. You can never have enough clean cloths, the contractor explains to Zach who looks in on his way to school and nips back home for an old T-shirt: every pass requires a fresh cloth or the white cement goes grey. Aline can't understand why they don't bring their own cloths. Takes her paintbox to the roof. Sketches in the watercolour pad with a soft pencil, old habit, keeping her hand in. Always that moment of anxiety when she does: is this just PlayDoh?

A shadow falls on her page.

It's the tiler's assistant from yesterday, the one who kept making eye contact. Mostly they don't, even those who stare; look back and they look away. This one holds your gaze.

He's offering her something, silently, because he knows she speaks another language. It's a painting he's unrolled from a sweat-cloth, and he'd like her to have it. First look at it and then keep it, it's hers. No, he doesn't want it back.

She looks. It's a festival of moss greens and cherry pinks. A woman at an upstairs window looking down on an empty court-yard; an old gatekeeper snoring at the open front door. Morning.

The remains of a storm flicker in the sky at one dark corner, but dawn rules. The painting is not recent, she can see that at a glance, but the colours are well preserved. Its mauves and greens, the startling amber of the watchman's tunic, thrill a palate given to primaries.

She looks back up at the giver. His silence imposes itself on her, so she replies in sign language. Are you sure? It's very beautiful. It's old. I can't take this from you. It must be worth a lot of money. Are you quite sure?

He is sure, she can see that. She looks down, sees her little paintbox. Will you take this? It's nothing, look just six colours. Do you like it? Yes! It's yours.

He's gone. Clutching the paintbox in the hand without the finger balloons.

Q uick

Zach is late. He's eating two lunches now, one to satisfy his old mother, and one with Aline. Sleeps in two beds too. He sets an odd five-tiered stainless-steel tower down on the table, frowning, her lunch in a tiffin carrier. Then remembers to kiss her. He'd like to examine her hand but he's too tired for that. Under his other arm he carries a sheaf of answer papers. Twice now Aline has seen this cool young man flustered. But he's just dealt with a fortune-teller who has a relative at the post office.

'They read your mail, pick out a significant date, and then come and want to read your palm.'

'What did he predict?'

'Your arrival.'

She laughs. 'Aren't they supposed to predict the future?'

'Ya. Bunch of crooks. I chased him off.'

'I saw you go to kick him.'

He grins. 'Just foxing. My hands were full. What's this?'

'It's a painting I was just given.'

He looks hard at her. What took her from the start was the quality of his attention: he listens with his whole being: his eyes, his hands, his knees are listening. Suddenly they're back in Peter and he's sitting on the floor with her examining another painting, listening. And she can't help but speak. She's been drawn out before, further than she meant to go, but never so disinterestedly. He disables the lie on your lips. Now he's waiting, leaning over the miniature.

'A man just came up and gave it to me. One of the workers.'

'What, just like that?'

'Yes. I was sitting on the roof and he appeared and gave it to me.'

'He didn't want you to buy it or anything?'

'No.'

'Strange. Maybe it was just for safekeeping.'

'Maybe. Or maybe he had to get rid of it. It looks pretty valuable. He was pretty adamant. It was *mine, mine.*' She repeats the gesture that accompanied the gift, an open-fingered roll of the hands as if pushing it away.

'He must fancy you.'

'I guess. He was kinda cute.'

Zach looks at her. He was joking, but now he sees that she would be immune to his ironies of class. She simply wouldn't see the social gap: a poor man, maybe, but a man. Whereas he sees another order of creature. For all her immense wealth she's closer to this worker than he could hope to be.

'Well, that was quick,' he'd like to say but is almost afraid to. So modifies it, on her terms to: 'You're not serious.'

She looks surprised, and leans over and takes his face between her hands. But even that response staggers him, because it's saying: why not? He pulls away, peeved in spite of himself. And at the same time aware that she's right, though can't she see it's not his fault he doesn't have two centuries of democracy behind him. In this country there are classes you'd be uncomfortable eating with let alone sleeping with.

'I do believe you're jealous!'

But even that note is wrong, the wording's wrong. It should be: You're not *jealous*! With a tinge of social horror he can recognize. This is a clear declaration that she loves him, Zach, but in a system of equivalences that could include this tiler's assistant.

'Silly boy! I want you.'

He's waylaid by contentiousness. 'For yourself.'

'Of course. I don't want you for *you*!'

'Sounds a bit like conquest.'

'Conquest is Everest, silly. I don't have anything to prove. Anyway, with conquest you don't go back. What am I doing here?'

She sways away from him and lets her head swing around to take in the new hemisphere and all its contents. What *is* she doing here? Then she sees he's still standing.

'Take a load off your feet.'

'Shall I tear him into little pieces?' He means the rival, not the fortune-teller. Then it occurs to him that maybe the fortune-teller meant the rival.

'Zachy.'

'Big pieces?'

'You can rip me apart.'

Even that he's too tired for. He sighs and sits down right there on the dining table. The sheaf of papers is still under his arm. He puts it down beside him, then picks it up again and drops it with a bang.

'Corrections,' he explains, following her glance. 'It's that time of year.'

'Are they correctible?'

'These are the tens. They're not even teachable. The younger ones maybe.'

'What do you teach them?'

'Scales. Do re mi. *I know where the Indians go*.'

She sings the childhood tune, in words she made up a long time ago. '*They go down to Tupelo*.'

He takes up the third line, softshoeing with his tomahawk, crumpling right up, the relief of it, '*There they dance and there they sing*,' and they do the last line together:

'INDIANS CAN DO ANY DAMN THING!'

'Can't do,' he laughs.

'Can do.' She's laughing harder. 'Hey, you're pretty lightfooted.' She's never seen him dance before; it's the first time she's seen him unbend with his clothes on.

'What's it *like*, the school?' He remembers that *like*; the last time it was Barista.

'Oh, very pretty campus.'

'And the teaching?'

'The seniors are the hardest. They're basically rich girls waiting to get married. To rich guys.'

'So what do they do?'

'Heckle. Hoot. Hump – not *me*. I'd lose my job.'

'And me.'

R *is for* R oof

See also R ed, R egal, R ibbon

R oof

The rooftop she loves.

She's never known a flat roof. Strolls up there at any time of day, a figure in red the locals have come to expect. The American. At home the penthouse has views to three compass points. Here, two floors up, you can look clear to the horizon in any direction, no blanks in steel and glass. Northwards are the highest mountains on earth, to the south a prefatory range of jagged hills; east and west the valley stretches with its roads and fields and housing colonies edged with forest. She must have measured the length of the roof a thousand times among the dragonflies and evening bats. Now and then a lone heron will flap overhead, white as a tablecloth, its yellow legs old fishknives. Zach's house, a single-storey structure, is just across the way, with two empty plots in between. She can see his study, can even see him at his desk late at night, and he can see her window where the new computer is set up; they exchange emails that bounce off a remote satellite when they could lipread if they really tried.

>*Come up for a spot of Double Dog?*
>*On my way.*

But he has to skip out, this mother's boy. The apron strings that extend to Seoul and Petersburg are shorter at home. How can A compete with someone who's cooked for this boy, sewn on buttons for him, who knows down to the last shred of ginger his food fusses, his cravings. She probably still makes his bed for him.

'Is she asleep?'

'I think so.'

'[*Does she make your bed for you?*] Any progress?' She means on the music he's working at.

'A bit.' He holds the glass up against the streetlight and jogs the ice cubes clad in whisky she claims is great. With its Panjab Distillery label of black and white Scotch terriers. He's not being terse and masculine; he just doesn't know how to tell her this time she's his muse. This piece is hers, these nocturnes. Because his nights are hers and everything in them. She's infected his dreams.

'Can you tell me something about it?'

'If you won't laugh.'

'Word of honour,' she laughs.

'It's a set of nocturnes. For you.' There, it's out.

'Zachy!'

She takes the glass out of his hands, puts it down, and kisses him slowly. He disengages himself, retrieves it and takes a sip.

'Nocturnes are supposed to be black. These are red. Well, dark red.'

Dark red is how she feels tonight. The way heat fills coal to glowing. He's been neglecting her lately. But suddenly she herself is distracted: she's remembered another tribute. Yesterday the tiler's assistant was back with a second painting. Not another miniature in pinks and greens. This one was his own work, a

simple frieze-like watercolour on card of a row of men following
a snakewoman. Done with her paints.

She wanted to ask Zach about the group; maybe tomorrow.
He's exhausted, she can see that, so lets him go home at one,
untouched.

The next night she mails him.

>*Punjab vodka?*
>*Don't blink.*

He's over so quick she's emboldened to tell him about the
new painting. He listens, his hands folded under his nose. Then
she tells him about the paintbox.

'He didn't touch the red.'

Z pours a Kremlin double.

'What did he touch?'

'The blue, the green, the brown, even the Chinese white. Everything but the red.'

'Mr Sombre.'

'Or Mr Picky. Give him credit. He stepped carefully around it.'

'Antichrist.'

She laughs. 'Well, yes, he's not Matisse.'

'Who is?'

'Right.' She looks down into her life as into a sewing box.
What is she? Where's that thimble of an identity? What could she
have done differently with her life? She looks up involuntarily at
Z. His life is still ahead of him. How to tell him just to live it? Take
him by the shoulders and say: *Look, just live? Fuck fame.* Or just
take him by the shoulders and take him? She does that and they
go down, there on the terrace, where the nosy neighbours could
see between the balusters if they were watching, but at the

crucial moment it's red she sees, not black. More wanting, not extinction. In his eyes too she sees the glint of an idea, as if this that they just did was grist to the mill.

They doze, their foreheads touching, wake to thoughts ten thousand miles apart. They were closer in Petersburg, close enough for mockery. 'Why New York, for godsake?' He's sharing her kitchen stool in the griffin mews, straddling her, counting off on his fingers Americans in Paris, that ignoble procession back to a finished world. 'Go paint Chillicothe!'

Now his finger beats time on her temple. She turns her head aside, breaks that light contact. Does he never stop? He'll go and miss his life – but who's she to warn him? All her life she's looked over her shoulder. *A line has just two dimensions*, the young woman at the mirror repeats; her name condemns her to flatness. Her father's choice, and then his shadow on top of that, but maybe also a certain lack of daring?

Well maybe she will go, somewhere. Else.

Z wakes suddenly desolate. Like a dog shaken out of sleep, he senses a departure and looks awkwardly at the nearest human for help. But she's turned over on her back now so they lie side by side, half stripped of clothes.

'What,' she asks him, putting him on the spot for a change, 'is music?'

He looks sideways at her. To you, he sees she means, so he returns to inspecting the velveteen sky and takes his time answering.

'It's a way out of silence,' he says at last. Not his private half silence, between the good and the bad ear, but the silence of space.

When he's gone home she lies awake in bed. For once she's pleased with his seriousness. It echoes her own notion of painting as a way out of darkness. She gets up and goes to the dresser and picks up the little painting the tiler's assistant gave her. Looks at it. His name on the back in careful Roman capitals: GILLU. She returns to bed and watches the sliding rectangles on the walls as cars go by, shapes on a magic-lantern wall. Her adult red was borrowed, she sees now, not even properly stolen; a colour must be won. As she falls asleep she dips a brush in infrared, watches it frizzle, hangs over its crazing, then loses balance and falls, tumbling, dropping down and down to that first bedroom on Eggleston under the maple shingle. If she can climb back into that cot and lie there and look, look with those eyes, she'll see.

Next morning she climbs to the mumpty. Sits. Catch the shape of last night's dream, trace out that dim outline, enter that silence. *Then I drew with my eyes shut.* Just that one precept, then forget Matisse. Dump him dead. She's quit the red room at last, that turbulent interior. Close your eyes. She empties her head of the clutter of a lifetime. It's a salon in there, more bric-a-brac than she ever imagined an independent spirit could collect. Shakes it out, dusts off and down and away. Squeezes a blob of black into her red and paints straight onto the page of her little sketch book. Her brush moving like an animate thing, a swift dark outline appearing, enclosing a familiar shapelessness, a white blur in the centre, a smear on a slide. She doesn't stop but recognizes the shape as it develops: it's herself, but as she would see herself with her lenses out. The head a bulge on a stalk, the trunk with its dangling limbs, a thumb where the brush twitched, a webbing at the stumpy feet, a gap between the legs where maroon bleeds.

Aline, only just there, everywhere and nowhere, but there. Was she meant to paint this one image, uncover this one truth, once? She puts the brush down.

R ibbon

In his room at the Hôtel Beaurivage in Nice, Matisse would place a red ribbon on the floor before the maid cleaned to mark where his easel stood.

Good morning, madame
Kindly note the ribbon
And step around it if you please

It marks a frontier (cross it at your peril)
Western civilization ends here
Or I like to think begins

Five hundred years it took to plot perspective
I demolished it in five minutes
All right ten years

Good morning Laurette
Must you peel off your glove in that fashion
Really it's too provocative even at this hour

RED

And please be more careful
The maid just found an earring
Under the pillow

You are too lovely for words
Lie down at once here on this rug
See the ribbon? Yes on it

All night it's hung in mourning on the doorknob
One leg on either side please
Makes it a road not a border

Wider please still wider
Wider (show me red)
God!

How can paint come close?

R egal

The Red Room didn't work in blue. Blue was the colour of the sombre *Conversation*, from the same year. There the Matisses confront one another like statuary with a window in between, neither party willing to budge an inch. She sits regally in black to the right, a calm but severe figure, who has just pronounced something incontestable. He stands very straight to the left looking her in the eye, about to reply. The word they have both chosen is wrought in iron on the balcony grille: NON.

Blue was also the colour of the great *Mme Matisse*, a painting Matisse included in his first major exhibition after some doubts, well founded as it turned out, about its reception. The critics, except Apollinaire, savaged it, especially the grey mask of a face, and yet a century on it is one of Matisse's strongest paintings. It is a formal masterpiece, but it is not a passionate declaration. The only warm colour in the painting, a layered work of thought upon thought, is a satiny yellow scarf with marmalade lights that winds through the many exquisite grades of blue – smoke, sky, aqua, indigo, turquoise, teal, and violet – to a straightout regal purple (that features also in the queenly enthroned figure in the *Conversation*, which drew on imperial Babylon), to enclose the seated figure in an almost protective gesture. It is a feature of great elegance too, almost a garter, worn over one shoulder and fallen halfway down the other arm, and its function is formal, reappearing like a talisman from behind the stiff figure to complete her gilding even as it unites within its girdle the various blues. All the same, blue rules the canvas from the background to the foreground. There is even a frosty blue seldom noticed at the tip of Madame Matisse's nose, the very point of that pale grey mask which the subject wept to watch slowly replacing what started out as a naturalistic version of her face. The nose hangs like an icicle with a drip in the middle of the mask, yet the figure is not in the least comical as it might so easily have become with its expressionless snowman-like impassivity. The face is one of immense gravity and pathos and the wintry figure owes much of its paradoxical allure to this surrounding strip of yellow. The scarf is a gesture of late gallantry as much as a decoration, an order, and also in compositional terms, a virtuoso piece of exquisitry.

But it is not a red ribbon.

That was reserved for M's models. Compared with the regal figures of these two blue paintings, the woman in *Madame Matisse in the Red Madras Turban* doesn't convince; she smiles with an almost childish uncertainty unbecoming of the selfpossessed woman in blue or the one enthroned in black, each regarded with complete and pitiless equality; in the red turban she counts on charm, not authority. She also wonders if she doesn't look a little silly. Red, she suspects, does not become her.

R ed

Red came to me this way no lie
with the astounding rightness of a black swan's beak
no guide in this dark grove   unless you count mother ghost   who hove
up and lingers still in linen closet   and scent
of violets

One day we cut the little bathroom short
ran up a wall because it looked straight in our hall
– *school*room – ma'am ghost keens – toilet attached for weans –
Cut it a hidden doorway   and where the old door was   hung shelves
were pantrified

I knew then as I drilled   stuck Rawlplugs   drove screws
sawed whiteskin particleboard   tacked red beading
what colour strove for that space   (and this)   so ran headlong
to Hurla hardware for a litre tin
of Signal Red

RED

One red they carried in acrylic and only one
not my dodgy haemoglobin red   mercurochrome or port
not scarlet crimson not poppy   not opticalmouse red not glorypea
nothing on the fancy shade card but
stopgo red

How it brushed on!   how it savaged white   rared from the tin
Ripped primer right off rendered brick   glued it straight back
Rang in my eye   rogered earhole   sucked bristle dry
Gorgeous gumptious randy red
How it sang!

Red ruled my life from beat to beat I knew
a bright thread ran from the heart   to the heart
the thin red line that kept me here   not boxed   no fear
so I might drink sun   crack open pomegranate
eat rubies

Red schooled the ape down from the trees   God wot
first stood for something else say   danger   keep off   hot
husbanded through black the genius of claret   next Raphael   next Spielberg
                                                    tame exotic parrot

lastly sad lingerie lust   small grist
for novelist

S *is for* S orry

See also S atyr

S atyr goatish woodland god; lustful man

Look at Picasso's *Satyr with Sleeping Nymph*.

An ink drawing in black and white, its drama of light and shadow seemingly divined in the actual moment of conception. It's a curious amalgam of loose sketch and crafted etching. The satyr, viewed side-on, half-kneels at the centre, arms outstretched in front of him in moonlight streaming through a casement, his Cretan head worked in great detail, as if it belonged to another picture altogether. The sleeping maiden's head is accomplished with three or four masterly strokes in the shadows of her lifted veil; she is not just asleep, she *is* sleep.

Sublimely achieved, full of astonishing effects, the sketch has an operatic formality. Consider the calm, even wooden, bearing of the satyr, the contemplative look on his face as his hands move like a dancer's towards the sleeping woman. The fingers of the reaching hand have just entered that most vulnerable space in the painting, the triangle between the breasts and the navel of the sleeping woman, the soft belly of her, bathed in moonlight, the same moonlight that falls on the the satyr from behind and shows his whole burly form. Now, at the instant of the sketch, he has crossed the boundary of her, while she sleeps on in bliss with her legs folded, bent at the knee, her buttocks and her sex facing the viewer, twice vulnerable.

But she's safe, you know. It's just a tableau. She is Sleep, he, the satyr, is – a model.

Matisse has a canvas on the same subject: *Satyr Approaching Sleeping Nymph*. The sleeping part is disputed. A. N. Izergina in my copy of a heavy Hermitage volume, a public-library discard ($1, thank you, Christchurch), believes she has just fallen, and points at the way her leg is in motion, still half in flight. I'm not sure: the arms suggest sleep, one outstretched but tucked under her head as she lies on the grass, the other bent with the elbow turned towards the viewer, its hand twisted under as only sleep (or else breaking) would allow. In any case, others have shown the painting's ancestry (the foreshortening echoes sleeping nymphs in Watteau and Poussin). This nymph's legs are simply there, stretched out; no private parts on display. She lies off centre in the foreground, with the fingers of one hand reaching out of the painting,

into our space.

The satyr is again centred. But here he is on his feet, his weight on one foot, the other leg stretched behind, only a toe on the ground. He is either running or taking one last menacing stride as he bends over the nymph. His gross hands overhang her. Again both are naked but here are no props, no sheets, no gauzy fabrics, no arched window, no balcony, no pot of herbs. Just grass, an undifferentiated body of water, and the truncated humps of three hills. And no streaming moonlight. Matisse has set this fearful assault in broad daylight. The horns, the beard, all the trappings of conventional satyry, of lust – all the excuses – are gone; here is a man about to rape. It is the most terrifying painting I know.

Picasso stages his encounter with a chiaroscuro that rivals his yet more dramatic *Minotauromachy* of the previous year, where the stage is full of actors and the source of light is, sentimentally, a flower girl's candle. In the *Satyr* etching and aquatint the moonlight-and-shadow is an artfully managed series of contrasts that stretches from the bright night outside through the satyr's curled tail and the nymph's smooth white thighs to the darkness of the room. But the very beauty of the setting, the speaking shadows cast by the balusters at the window, the many textures and planes, distract from the crucial encounter.

Picasso's model will get up and walk away, but in Matisse there's no escape. The figure that hangs over the nymph on the grass will hang there in eternal menace. A wide even light floods the scene from every side with its pitiless glare. The choice of a bucolic emerald green for the entire background only serves to accentuate the terror: this is a daytime attack. The landscape has outlines but no shading, no shadows, not a single stone on the grass for relief; there's nowhere to hide. Even the nymph's body is represented in the flat, with scarcely any modelling of the pale pink skin. Only the hunched man (no tail, no horns) has his underside tanned. The darkest shadows in the painting are under his forehead in the hollows of his eyes, and his hair is a shock of black that is like a hole in the canvas.

If anything can save the nymph it's the daub of red-gold hair on her head, hung there like a magic fleece. The painter had red hair himself; he's on her side, holding that hand.

A novelist's fancy? Here is Picasso himself on Matisse.

'If there is some red spot in one of my paintings it is unlikely to be the heart of the work. You could remove the red and still the painting would be there. But in Matisse's work it is inconceivable that you could remove a spot of red, no matter how small, without the entire painting instantly collapsing.'

Classically nymphs and satyrs were in the game together. They prance through countless paintings from antiquity on; they are the Chase in human guise. It was always harder on the nymph when the game got rough, which it was always about to. But Matisse has humanized mythology by removing the trappings of that chase. A few years earlier he had done a conventional version of the same subject in glazed tile. There the satyr is horned and bearded; he even has a mischievous smile. Shorn of those props the game turns serious. Now it's a question of power, of naked force. Of domination and submission, which can still be a game, but one where the line is in the last instance invisibly drawn. It is as if Matisse, who spent countless hours working with nude models, were musing on one possible relation between himself and them. As if this work were not entitled *Satyr Approaching Sleeping Nymph* or even *Satyr and Fallen Nymph* but merely *The Artist and his Model*.

Compare the most brutal renditions among Goya's war etchings, say, the unforgettable corpse impaled on a branch. I shrink every time from the artist's unflinching presentation, but it's a response of horror, not fear. The damage is done, the pity spent; there is everything to loathe and nothing to fear. In *Satyr Approaching Nymph* the future is open, as open as the space in which the action is always about to happen; I can't step back, there's no escape. There is only fear, and one saving dab of red.

Compare one last painting where a woman is in imminent danger, Balthus' *The Window*. A young woman, squarely at the centre of that canvas, her blouse wrenched so one breast is bare, retreats to the sill of an open window at roof level, one hand raised above her head in terror. As in the Matisse, the artist is a palpable presence just outside the painting, but where Balthus himself (and by extension, even by invitation, the viewer) appears to be the attacker, Matisse is here almost as guardian angel, his brush dipped in saving red. It is as if Matisse the painter were aware of the worst he as a man could do to this model naked in front of him, and stepping back a long way past civilization, as far back as humanly possible, he accuses not just all art but nature.

Satyr Approaching Nymph hung in Shchukin's Matisse room in Moscow in a setting of respectable parlour furniture and drapery; the well-bred but troubled millionaire who had the male genitalia in Matisse's *Music* painted over to preserve decorum may have asked the painter to reposition the satyr's groping left arm for a like reason. And Matisse may have agreed, recognizing that decorum might be one answer to a question he seems to address from the *Conversation* on: can one be alone with a woman and not bedevil her?

S orry

Aline's eyes open in the dark.

There's somebody in the room.

She goes rigid where she lies, listens on every side, scanning the darkness. No, not here. But there is someone out there. Trying to get into the house. *No!* Now what? She lies there flooding with adrenalin, just her eyes moving as she strains to listen. She didn't mean to go to sleep, must have rolled over and turned off the light. Her instinct is to turn it back on but fear tells her not to and she can't move anyway. The noise seemed to come from across the hall, where the room she uses as a study is. She left her computer on in there and came to bed meaning to read for a bit but fell asleep. It feels late, like she's slept heavily. The noise that woke her was twofold, a click as of iron meeting wood and then a back and forth rasp that could be a cricket or could be a bolt being worked.

Silence.

Now a new sound, softer and more alarming, of stealthy movement. Inside. O my god. She slides one foot along the bedsheet and over the edge of the bed where her slippers are. Sits up inch by inch, afraid the bed will creak, then rises very slowly and moves to the bathroom. Bolts herself in and stands there breathing. What she needs to do is unbolt the door into the yard and slip out. But out where? What if there's someone out there too?

She sits down on the john with her face in her hands. Could it have been the fridge motor knocking? Or the battery wall clock above the mantel? She stands up and lifts her wristwatch, which costs more than this house, to catch a shaft from the yellow streetlight. The watch, so familiar by day, looks utterly uncon-cerned; its second hand sweeps the black face, remote as a satellite, skimming yellow diamonds that could be distant stars. She feels a spasm of hatred for it, for this object she has always trusted, felt closer to than any other, which now proves indiffer-ent to her fate. But offers a reading: half-past two.

Was it a dream? She remembers Zach saying the other night that the worst in history and the best in art happens between three and four in the morning. The thought of him calms her; she's imagining things. It might even be him.

She considers a moment then eases back the bolt on the door and returns to the bedroom. Listens hard at the door to the hall then steps out of her slippers and crosses barefoot under the clock, moving cautiously by the light of a red bead on the fridge and a blue bead on the voltage stabilizer. She already knows the geography of the furniture, but she's unaccustomed to a stone floor all through the house. Her toes splay further on this sexy polished surface; she feels shorter but also fleeter. She could run if she had to, but where?

The fridge comes on with a jolt as she passes and she jumps but steadies herself on its handle. The faint light of the computer coming from her studio reflects off the floor ahead, an astral glow that fills the room and sifts through the door. The curtain is billowing gently: she must have left the fan on too. She pictures the room as she approaches, the black window of the starflight screensaver on the desk, the fan blades turning overhead, pages fluttering under paperweights, mute patient objects in a half-furnished room awaiting her return. The curtain hem flaps to show her something else.

A naked foot.

The wadding of flesh where heel and sole meet the floor, the jutting ankle bone, and the curve of the calf above. Facing the other way, so she steps back at once, then sideways out of the line of the door. As she does she sees a reflection in the glass of the studio bookcase. She knows that profile, the spatulate jaw, as if the head had been squeezed from above and below in delivery.

It's the tiler's assistant. Staring fixedly at the screen, mesmerized by the black vortex of an endless journey through space. And as if the moment of her recognition snaps a thread in his vision, the head whips around to look over his shoulder. At once she retreats but a joint cracks somewhere in her foot and the sound is confirmation.

He knows he's been seen and darts behind the curtain. She thinks he's gone, out the window, but forgets windows have grilles here. So goes forward, not back. When she enters the room he's still there, in the corner, very still, bashful even, since he is more than half naked. Naked except for a loincloth and smeared in some kind of blacking and grease that catches the glow of the computer screen. He looks up at her, his hands lifted so the yellow palms face her, fingers apart and pushing the empty air between them. Not the rolling downstroke of the fingers that accompanied the gift of the painting but all the fingers upright in a steady back and forth buffer action that says both *Keep back* and *I'm not here to harm you*.

She stops where she is, makes no attempt to move but instinctively repeats the rapid reassuring wag of his chin onto which she can't help but graft the hopeful semblance of a smile that's partly of her culture and partly as old as hospitality, as if to say *It's all right, but* – with its nervous subtext: *what happens now?*

He smiles gratefully in return, and picks up something he let fall on the desk and puts it back down a little further away, as if to say OK, here it is back. It's the miniature he first brought her. He nods half at the screen in acknowledgement of the device that waylaid him, held him bound by its hypnotic eye. He's never seen a computer screen close up, and still can't tell what this one's doing with its stream of stars.

This, he signals, *ensnared me*, indicating the screen that drew him in, but the words come out garbled even in his own language, so he gives up and simply steps back up to the desk, turns again to the screen, submitting to its spell to show her what happened. And is caught up again in spite of himself, so it's no longer a reenactment but a mystery all over again, the way the stars keep getting born at the centre and streaming outwards to the edge of the frame and past you on every side in the dark room.

She leans against the wall, one foot on the other, watching him there, his angular body rigid under the white sheen, his eyes soft in contemplation. Rapt in a way she can remember from the first time she saw the display herself, so she's standing there again entranced. He breaks the spell and steps back now into the chair which rolls away on its castors, more magic. He gives it another light push with something like a boy's amusement, and sits down in it as if in a car, and pushes back gently, test-driving it, bending over to look at the wheels. Then looking full up at her with a broad smile that vanishes suddenly when his eyes take in for the first time her bare arms and shoulders, her feet.

Now it's her turn to feel naked and she sees what it does to him and the way he acknowledges that too with a helpless shrug and a new gesture that opens both hands palms upward like moth wings parting. She can't help the way she's feeling either, the relief flooding her and the new turn to the old substances churning in the blood, directing her from some dark centre till it seems unnatural not to step towards the chair, her black-smeared chair, she can't help but notice, and climb onto him with her back to the unstoppable procession of stars, as she thinks: *Sorry, Zachy.*

T *is for* T iffin

See also T hrills, T intinnabulation, T ongue

T iffin

'They're like a sect. Or a secret society. Or maybe just dacoits, but they're generally not armed.' Mrs Wilding has a schoolmarm's passion for definition, will refine and refine till she gets it right. 'They break in naked, in just the shorts, and their bodies oiled so they're hard to catch if you do grab them.' Aline has a bizarre picture of the old lady wrestling with a greased bandit. She's come to enjoy her visits as much as her cooking, which arrives every day in the hotcase.

'Dawl curry,' Mrs Wilding smiles her satisfaction. 'Today you get to try Anglo-Indian khana. You're not a vegetarian, are you?' She spits out the word, giving each syllable equal and contemptuous stress. 'With curry leaf from our garden.'

'Curry leaf?'

'The sweet neem. Dawl curry's not dawl curry without it. Imagine! Down south we used to pay through the nose for it and here it grows wild. You must come and see my herb garden.'

'I'm an inconvenience to you,' Aline offers.

'No trouble at all.' Mrs Wilding puts the tiffin carrier on the dining table. 'If I'm busy the servant girl will deliver it.'

She turns away with a catsmile. But you won't get my son, born on Ash Wednesday.

T ongue

He never tires of the sound of her tongue. Not the sound of the strange words: those he can accept as foreign and inaccessible; not the tone: the pig girl has hers and he has his and everyone has his peculiar register, but the music of this language, so different from his own and the pig girl's and anyone's he has ever met. The way her sentences can go up at the end as if she were asking a question when he knows she's simply stating something; the way her syllables dib down unaccountably or huddle or run on; even the sounds that have no words attached: the fat soft nuzzle of her laugh, to his ear slightly masculine, the sliding note of dismay, the two-tone uh-huh of her agreement when she approves of something he has done.

She stares like a child at his lips as they move, as if hanging on the slightest movement will make the meaning plain, but finally stretches her own mouth in a baffled smile and sweeps her head as if to brush the incomprehension aside and with it all her past. She's never felt so free, not even when she parachuted in on Zach. Released, her chin will bob right back, but now the smile is a wide wild wicked embrace that triggers his high-pitched cackle. Then his quick slide into dark watchfulness. It's an alertness without expectation; she remembers that from before he approached her. He was the one with a red handkerchief tied on his head who sat apart on the workers' lunch hour and simply watched the world the way he's watching her now, with animal neutrality. It's the opposite of her husband's distracted glance, every look an enterprise. With Zach it's entreaty; earnestness hobbles his looking. G's gaze is open, tenanted but unconstrained and unconstraining. When he's looking he's looking. When he's sitting as he is now wrapped in a fresh towel, his, she's tried to show him, but a towel is common property where he lives, he's sitting. His whole person sits. Such a towel he's never seen. He fingers the pile as if that is all that matters in the world. Not futures, not reputation, just those delicious springy strands of looped cotton. He looks up from them – they've gone. Now she exists and she alone.

So they look at each other for minutes together till he pulls on the T-shirt and jeans she gave him and makes to go and she jumps up and blocks the way and gives him her tongue and the madness begins again.

So he's unprepared for seriousness when she pushes him away one day and starts to mime. A crazy string of gestures he can't figure out, ending with a heavy makeup session, like she's in a beauty parlour getting her face done.

His jaw drops and shifts sideways into an admiring smile.

She wants to get sooted. She wants to go along on a smudge! Tonight?

T hrills

Imagine him standing by your bed in the dark.

Studying you. Perfectly still, hardly breathing. His eyes half shut so you don't see the whites, but studying you closely as you sleep, every part of you with his night vision.

No magic, all it takes is application. Like tasting the sugars in grass, prickle of salt in millet, trace of lime in artichoke.

Close your eyes and look at black. Shut out all light, even the faintest ash of starlight, let the X-ray print of windows subside, drown yourself in darkness. Mine the dark now. Pick at the stubborn coalface, think only of the black seam in front of you, don't pray the roof stays up, don't think of your lover. Look for cracks in the vein where leaf lay upon leaf for aeons before turning coal, don't think of the aeons. When you see the first hairline, black on black, frozen lightning, you're almost there. One by one, mineral glints appear in the surface, the coalface wakens, reveals hatches, hallways, wells and silences.

Now open your eyes – *not* wide. A streetlamp could blind you. Sparks where the cricket fiddles, every latch a flashbulb. Just a slit this time.

See?

RED

He sees the room you sleep in lit from a hundred angles, watches you sleep under a battery of arc lights. Sees a plain watch on your husband's wrist. Lets him turn, lets his eyelids open, the eyeballs roll back up again. Never looks a sleeping man in the eye. You turn towards him in your sleep, bangles tinkling, he waits, lets you settle. Crouches down and brings his face up close to yours. You mumble, fuss with the pillow, your hand falls . . .

. . . on his shoulder *Mother of the snakefolk!* He freezes.

Your hand gropes in the dark, your darkness, his light, your sleeping fingers find a strange new bone, hair where your husband has none, and now you dream in earnest while he squats unmoving, swiftly scanning your neck, your wrists, your ankles.

Which one's gold, Gilgitan, which one's silver? Hurry she's waking come on wrist or neck now which? He needs just one burst of light to tell him, one tiny searchlight off button or hook. Or tooth – *yes*, the necklace, *gold!*

He slips a finger under it, into your open-mouthed dream of kissing that flesh, returns the kiss, tugs gently, keeps your spittle, tugs little harder, but now you've got his alien scent, you open your eyes, look into that mask an inch away.

His eyes ream your head.

She's awake. There, it's off, now go! He palms the necklace, turns on one foot.

God, a ghost!

Aline is standing there in the bedroom doorway, watching.

Not where he left her in the shadows at the open back door by which they came in. Her eyes shine like lamps, but brighter still are the teeth which show her mouth twisted in a hungry grin. He grips her wrist hard, so hard it hurts, like he means it to for disobeying him, and tugs once sharply, a tug that means many things, come, come now, come with me you beauty, but mostly, let's go.

Dogs! Where'd they come from?

Run! Run, you crazy bitch! Run for your life! This way, over here. Here's a knee-up. Put your foot here, up, over the wall, now jump. *Jump*, you cunt! Don't look back, just run!

RUN!

T intinnabulation

Programme notes to Work in Progress: To infuse space into
sound, flesh out a spatial extension to music. 26 nocturnes,
one for each alphabet.

*T*intinnabulation (Number 20).

Days after his mistress has returned to her husband's house,
the lover finds a toe ring under the bedside table, and suddenly
remembers with bell-like clarity the moment of its falling: the
pitch and character of a sound only now identified and made
clear, so the two moments, of puzzlement and of understanding,
though separate in time join and become one. This experience he
translates into spatial music: the effect of one whole dimension,
depth or distance in time, suddenly cancelling itself out and
returning, facet by facet, to the one single plane of infinite
extension. Trumped, the third dimension gives back depth, all
fertile space, into his safekeeping as it opens out like released
origami collapsing to a single sheet of paper.

The performance has rings, toe rings, bangles, and other
ornaments rising and falling above a bed, suspended by nylon
fishline and picked out by spotlights against a backdrop of black.
Bed, bedside table, lamp, all black on stage with the blacked
performer; a copper coil wound about the glowing red cross-

sectioned mattress. Marina Tsvetaeva's *An attempt at jealousy* read out as a sporadic current passes through the coil and the innersprung mattress lights up like a block of wired ice. Every time a ring falls, the tinkle is amplified so the audience can hear it. The sound is prerecorded on a stone floor.

Zach pencils a full stop and chucks the page aside. Done! Now *live*! Life's been on hold while he musicked. He dials up BSNL and types a Zee*bytes* message:

>*OK for a spot of nooky?*

After eight days of silence the mail is a surprise. She knows he's been up to his ears in work, and it's just as well, considering, but still can't help feeling, even after all that's happened to cancel out what was between them, a touch of annoyance at his neglect of her.

>*Don't see you from up here any more*, she replies.

She can't, like she used to, from the roof but knows he hides away in his bedroom, a pillow over his good ear because Mrs W's TV's turned up high. She knows the nocturnes are for her but is still piqued that he can spend his nights musing next door. She knows she's been busy herself and must come clean about ... him. She realizes she doesn't use her lover's name. He's never asked her hers and she can manage, it seems, without his. The very notion of names is a daytime fantasy and she no longer sees him by day.

So she ends:

>*Sorry, Zachy, access denied, username invalid.*

U *is for* U ncle

See also U nwired, U ndeceived

U ncle

Uncle is the new leveller. *Sir* has gone out the window, the way of *babuji*. Good. Good riddance. In the new Dariya Dun it's uncle and aunty for anyone in the street older than you. Uncle, says the young man at the gate, do you need rubber hose for your gas cooker? Uncle, says the man at the crossroads (my own age I would have thought), which way is Dharampur?

Democracy. Not a gowned manly Pre-Raphaelite with red hair. This one has black hair, though a bad diet has left the tips mouse-brown. The eyes are not yet dimmed, mouth laughing as it heckles a truant piglet, teeth bright from chewing stolen sugarcane. A face to mail God about.

To: Lord of the Sties
Subect: Not fair

>*Where does she leave the rest of us, Old Spoiler?*

peeled switch in hand	*pig girl passes*
red cellophane cap	*is anyone lovelier than me?*
never such a noon	*air so sweet*
sowsnout in truffle	*toesquelch in mud*
and uncle just gave me	*fridge water*

U ndeceived

Zach's teeth bare in a guilty grimace when he reads the message, but he won't have it. *Access DENIED*! He'll go show her *denied* right now.

Right then the power fails: his UPS whistle blows and the battery clicks on. He must go back and scroll through and sort out his accidentals in the next ten minutes or lose the day's work. When he lifts his eyes from the screen it's dark outside. A general blackout, not just houses but streetlights too, so stars are suddenly visible in a corner of the window. He's been meaning to get an inverter, mostly for his mother; himself he quite likes the kerosene lamp with its curly-wurly glass chimney, very twentieth century.

'Dark times,' comes his mother's voice, unperturbed. She knows better than to blunder about looking for matchbox and candles. 'If you wait long enough they go away.'

'"Now in British times",' he starts her off helpfully.

She nods into the dark and takes the cue: 'we didn't know what a power cut was.'

'And most people didn't know what power was.'

'True.' She has a schoolmarm's passion for fairness. 'Did you lock the gate?'

RED

A loaded question. It means: *So your old mother doesn't get murdered in her bed.* And: *You're not going anywhere tonight, are you, my only son?*

'And helpmeet.'

'Beg your pardon?' Anglo mothers.

'Nothing.' When the gate is locked he goes up onto the roof instead and waits for the power to come back on. It obliges almost immediately. All around windows appear, blue and yellow and white squares, as starlight dims. Cheers from the teenager next door who was watching one-day cricket.

Aline's not in her studio, but the light is on. He saw her last night after a whole week and she was behaving strangely then. Should he feel guilty or outraged?

He goes back down, composing a sharp answer to her mail but a melody, beauty, waylays him on the stair, something in the screech owl's shuffling cry, and by the time his foot's on shingle he's inside a nocturne, not the night. He works till three, checks at his mother's door to make sure she's breathing, then goes back up onto the roof to stretch.

She's there! Aline's window is the only square of light on at this hour. She sits at her screen, her hair a red daub in yellow colourfield. It's like *The Red Room* reversed, so you're looking *in* the Issy window at the maid. He sees her with new eyes and feels the sting of fresh desire. He can see her lips move, could reach out and touch her. If he cupped his hands right and whispered she'd hear him. He listens with his head on a tilt to the luscious seedpod ripple of her keyboard; she's playing for him, could twist his head off with a note completely new. But he senses a reproach in the turn of her shoulder, the same that he last read in her eye: *where*, she seemed to be asking, is that charmer of Petersburg?

Or for that matter the stud? She can't recognize this sullen moody man.

He turns brusquely aside and picks up the drip of a tap into a cistern three houses away. Five notes: five sufficient, unregardful notes, true as pebbles. Precisely what he needs to cleanse the murky passage he thought to brighten superficially with xylophone. As it stands prepared piano clomps through a melody of six notes; what it needed was this clarity. Coming as it does on the heels of discord. He thinks back to Petersburg. He's just reeled in from her griffin mews and lectured the astonished horns on beauty when: enter the daughter on her mission of rupture! Maybe they *are* joined, back to back, confusion and peace? Can sound reconcile opposites? The way the overflow from the neighbours' roof tank falling thirty feet onto concrete sounds like fire crackling up through brushwood. He stops in his tracks. There: it's happened again. I've left her behind. He shakes his head. If he could only be still, like water in an underground place.

And right then, yet again, he's distracted.

He's back in the Hermitage on the last day, nipped in to take one last look at the thirteenth-century madonna with her laser blue and her dove.

She's there too, of course, Red; this time she's waiting for him, has followed him clear across to the medieval gallery, to this Virgin in blue.

'Hey, look, I'm sorry about yesterday.'

'So am I.' He means he wishes he hadn't stopped when he did, but knows she's talking about the invasion.

'We spoilt your music.'

'No, you didn't, you *made* it.'

'Look, if I can make it up to you in any way. I have friends.'

She means in high places. She has money too, and is young enough to brag.

'Not the mafia?' he smiles.

She takes him up, jerks a thumb down at the Neva. 'No concrete gumboots? One size fits all. But seriously.'

'Seriously?'

'Word of honour.'

'You can steal me that.' He points at the kneeling Virgin. It's small enough to fit under her cape, big enough to ring every alarm bell in the house.

She looks back at him, very straight and still and stern. If he could be as still as that.

'I will.'

He takes her face in his hands and admonishes her. 'You won't.'

'I will.'

'Just don't.'

He leads her away with a parting glance at the Virgin. Down in Dvortskaya she takes his hand. They walk in silence across the great square. Halfway across he feels a squeeze.

'Hey, thanks for, like, what you didn't do.' She means at the Hilton, what everyone else does to her, with her. She sees a friend in the distance and drops his hand. Time to go. 'You know, I wish you were my old man.'

Well, *Metronome* got his age wrong too, the other way. He can hear N chuckling. Swings and roundabouts, young Zach, swings and roundabouts.

She waves and smiles and turns again and calls across the square. '*Sure* there's nobody you want bumped off?'

He walks up and down the roof keeping an eye on Aline's

window with its older, redder head and deep breathing and rolling his shoulders the Dr Siddiqui way, thinking: tomorrow, I'll make it up to her tomorrow. With what? Flowers? Chocolates? He looks around as if he were in a mall, then stops and smiles. He's trying to bribe the richest woman in the land. He looks up at the sky. The Great Bear's climbed high up a black branch above the pole star, the wheel of night turned half a round since he was last up here.

Bedtime.

Just as he's turning away he sees a shadow cross the empty plot and leap the wall into Aline's yard and disappear around the house. He's so startled he's tempted to jump straight down onto the portico roof and go rap on her window. He waits a moment, bristling all over.

Then he sees her head turn as if she hears a noise behind her. But she doesn't hold it there as she would if she were listening intently. Her body says she's heard a familiar sound, and in fact she rolls back on her chair in confirmation, pushing away from the desk and tilting her chairback so her head's bent right over, looking up at somebody.

Somebody bends over her and kisses her mouth then comes around and straddles her lap. And Zach is falling down a shaft where there is no light at the bottom, just black knowledge oozing and a sudden heat that's scorching everything in its path.

U nwired

I am trying to conceive of the tens of thousands of messages that crisscross the middle air, this air, every single second. Stinging rebuttals, tepid yeses, round noes, pulsing along jellyfilled cables then flashing through this private space on their way from device to device. Never mind the air: they're passing through my *head* – someone else's nameless traceless passion earwigging my brain – and I'm oblivious of their passage. This walled garden, so tranquil and green, with its pomegranate and peach, its moss-darkened walls where squadrons of black dragonflies park at peace, is awash with electronic signals, radio waves, and stringy matter, a humming crossroads of love and spite and barter and betrayal. Impossible to truly credit this bazaar of lies and breaking news, reports that riddle these walls and this very body without so much as a tremor of spidersilk. It's like a parallel universe, sealed off, unshareable, unknowable, and perhaps just as well.

Olivia's latest message got here while we slept, I well, Manda not so well because her mattress is carded cotton and unsprung, not a Sealy. The Aztec is not coming, yet. I tell Manda but she seems too full of the present to care. No TV but she has a laptop, a Walkman, and a short-wave radio: am I an ogre? Books. Lately she's been going to Hindustani vocal music lessons with her friend and comes home to practise her *sa re ga* through the afternoon.

'What's wrong with mornings?' she wanted to know the first day. 'Guruji says, "Rise early and practise with a calm and rested mind when lungs and throat are clear."'

'You will clear your throat in the afternoon when *I'm* fully rested,' I rule. Fathers are governments and you don't always get the kind you deserve.

She looks upset but my Manda never sulks. And her reward is a surprise visit from Zach with whom she can talk music till the yaks come home. The surprise for me is he's alone, but I save my questions till Manda is indoors stewing up a pot of Indian tea with cardamoms.

'She's busy,' he says lightly, but can see I'm not deceived. 'I'm not her keeper,' he tries next, but I keep my eyes fixed on him. *Where is Aline?* He changes the subject to the man who was executed last week for the rape and murder of a fourteen-year-old girl. I listen with one ear cocked for Manda. Zach is our newspaper and our television but right now I can only wish he'd change the subject.

'What crime?' Manda asks balancing the tea tray down the front steps.

'Rape,' Zach answers matter-of-factly.

I could strangle him. I'm furious that he should even utter the word in front of her. *Im*becile! Say that again and I'll kill you.

He looks at me as if he heard every word I spoke. A little puzzled by my rage until he sees my point of view. Then he's faintly amused by the rabid prudery behind it; N, old son, his eyes say, she *knows* the word. Every girl knows it from the age of reason on. The fact that he's right is no comfort.

'It really wouldn't *hurt* to have a TV, you know, Papadumb,' Manda says when Zach is gone. 'If only for the news.'

'*Especially* not for the news, you silly girl!' It's not the world I'm trying to shield her from but the grim enchantment of the well informed. But I can't be bothered explaining. I'm still smarting from Zach's indiscretion.

She goes off to her room and practises her fingering on the harmonium we picked up at Pratap's. For half an hour her mellow scales fill the house, soothing my spirit.

At dinner I make amends by telling her I got my first guitar at the same music shop a hundred years ago.

She looks scandalized: 'Why not a sitar!'

I tickle the air and croon. 'Just a poor Anglo strumming on his guit, men.'

'Not funny.'

V *is for* V irus

See also V ertigo, V an Gogh

V irus

Thousands of kinds but this one is particular, launched by an enemy. Configured to attack any file in which the word *red* appears. Word has got out. So every alphabet in this abecedary (thus far) is corrupted; each was a separate file. Also, quite needlessly, others with words that might include the formation *red*. So: kindred, predator, and so forth, even proper names such as Modred and Reddy. Mindless energy on the rampage. For weeks, months, I've been warned to save, meaning to save, onto a disk, a floppy. Procrastination, but also faith, unfounded as it turns out, but also, most insidious of all, belief. Belief in one's centrality, one's specialness. One's invincible immunity to fate.

Here is a coincidence. Just this morning an acquaintance called, much too early, and hearing the word *fate* crop up in the fog of half-awake conversation I began to think, even as she talked, of a story to be called *The Fate Healer*. A man who for a consideration will take you by the shoulders and turn you a few degrees off course, off the track of your given fate. A remaker of destinies. How the trick is done is the crux of the story, but little did I know as I sat there rubbing the sleep from my eyes that I would need just such a healer before the end of the day.

'Just clicking on Explorer is enough,' the surdy engineer says lifting his finger, after a grave lecture on the perils of unprotected surfing.

'I will never again click on Explorer. Cure me this once.'

He holds out the hard disk, an embossed runic plate engraved in Bangalore under conditions of sterility only remote planets achieve. Somewhere in that inscrutable lump is my manuscript, riddled with the pox.

'It's like genetics,' he says. 'One dot of DNA is wrong here and you come out with six fingers there.' He points at his foot, meaning toes; the words the same in his language. I nod foolishly and he sees I haven't understood a thing.

'Nothing is certain,' he smiles his sad smile and kickstarts his scooter. On the subject of Not Saving he will not condescend to speak.

'Spare me this time,' I address God after many years, when the surd is gone. 'I'll brush up on computing, I'll do a course. What *exactly* is this worm?'

'Look. It's like your novel,' He says. Like the surdy, He can't take my profession seriously. 'One iota of infection here and a character can take a wrong turn there.'

I nod intelligently but can see he sees through me. So I stop quibbling. 'Look, just spare the book and you can have anything you like.'

'Anything at all?' In this bargaining mood He sounds like the Devil. 'I could ask for what you love most.'

At the moment what I love most is in already in jeopardy, the book, so it seems an academic issue. But at that moment Manda slips into the room looking for the pencil-sharpener.

'Why don't you have your own!' I shout, as enraged as a father whose daughter has slipped purdah. What's she doing exposing her face to a stranger?

She looks at me surprised. 'All right, all right!'

And stalks off, too late.

A cough. It *is* the Devil.

'*Anything?*'

I'm sitting at my desk, head in hands. I look the other way at the computer tower that swallowed up my manuscript. Suddenly I'm visited by a fierce longing for the old days of pencil and paper. Why, why, was I persuaded to change? I can see the cloven foot, tapping. I throw up my hands.

'Anything.'

V an Gogh

Matisse knew better than to mix red and black. He lived to ninety-two. Van Gogh didn't: he died at thirty-seven.

It is the year 1889. Vincent Van Gogh is sitting in the garden of the hospice Saint Remy. The sun is going down. Last year he painted *Moored boats* in full sunshine. But follow for one moment the tubby man in that painting trundling a wheelbarrow down the gangplank. Suddenly this canvas bathed in sunlight, the famous light of the south, begins to shake, the yellow to sicken, the green of the water to grey. The whole plank heaves and bucks: this is drowning water. Check: could he swim? There are no books here, no libraries in this one-horse Dariya Dun. I must rely on reproductions, on downloads, on photocopies sent me by friends. (One librarian in Calcutta refused to allow the Matisse nudes to be copied.) So who is to tell me if Van Gogh could swim? No matter. In 1888 he's already drowning.

But now it's 1889, his last year. He is painting the canvas that will come to be known as *The Hospital Grounds at Saint Remy* when he sees a new colour. He sees, he writes to Emile Bernard, 'a ray of sunshine, exalted into orange, dark ochre ... you will understand that this combination of red ochre, green saddened with grey, black strokes encircling the outlines, this produces a little of the sense of anguish which often afflicts certain of my unfortunate comrades, and which is called black-red.'

Nobody has caught, nobody before him has tried to identify, the colour of anguish.

Black-red.

V ertigo

Aline sits on the roof taking in her favourite view. Across the way there's a date palm silhouetted against the sky with a storm of red behind it where the sun just went down. A host of crows are flapping above it, cawing and zigzagging in the red air. Other crows from other colonies are making their way in ones and twos overhead to join the melee. What can it be, she wonders, then realizes what it is.

It'll be the flying ants she saw yesterday in the front yard, rising into the evening air. She got a close look at them as they swarmed up out of holes in the ground, an endless stream, unhurried but unstoppable, like creatures off an assembly line. With their drone-like bodies and outsize wings they did look cumbersome and manufactured. They came up out of the darkness bewildered and circled the hole timidly, tentatively. Light and pitiless open air closed in on them as they looked for courage in a world ten seconds old. One by one, they shook out their wings and worked them without conviction, and obedient to some inner dictation took heavily to the air. The first few individuals she lost sight of straight away until she learnt to track them in their awkward circling flight, then she lost those too in the general swarm. A fork-tailed blackbird swooped down off a wire and took one in flight, then another and another, easy pickings. Today it's the crows' turn.

She watches the slaughter around the palm tree in the dimming light. At this distance the ants are invisible but she can imagine their laboured flight through the new element. From the time of their emergence into the open air they have perhaps a minute before a crow gets them. One minute of freedom within the necessity that propels them, one minute of light, now a gorgeous crimson to her eye, then the black beak of fate. What happens to those who get away, she wonders? They can't rise very far. Night and distance envelop them, and surely their wings must tire of the world.

She turns away from the spectacle of the crows towards the darkness that has already fallen everywhere except in that little patch by the palm tree. With her the theorem was reversed: moments of necessity within a larger freedom. Twice now she's obeyed a dictation that seemed to come from a long way down in the blood, and already she's tired, of her wings, almost of the world. Already the excitement of this dark fortnight of the moon has begun to thin. She can bring herself to see, if not yet say, that she will tire of her new lover. Isn't it time she simply quit, while everyone's ahead? It seems right, or ripe, if one can speak of right conduct in the circumstances. What does conduct mean to creatures obedient to their fate?

A wobble in her stomach, like vertigo.

Smudge night tonight. The last one. No more after this.

Little flitting bats have now joined the fray as it gets too dark for the crows. The crows give up, go home. Flying foxes lured from their high straight paths glide down into a passing flutter then piously resume their measured flap, aligned once more with the phantom of a distant tree.

W *is for* W itch

See also W alled Garden, W ired

W ired

He's late.

They're doing the house next door. Smudge the Last. There's a leering boy Aline dislikes there, and a father who's worse. Tonight is at her request, not to take anything, just to scare them shitless. Aline checks the time in the watch on the dressing table. He won't let her wear it, anything that might glitter. A single glint reveals you, can jeopardize a smudge.

Darkness has fallen.

She looks in the mirror and can't help but smile. Blackface doesn't suit her. She looks like a rag doll, the golliwog with red hair she may have had as a child. Did she? It's all too far away now in the past. Her youth is history, never mind childhood. She sees it not in the mirror but in their eyes, Z's, G's, in the respect that can't help but tinge their looking. It's time she went home anyway. Not to Richard and his Armani face, the eyes focused just past you on his next billion. Maybe to Red, who's surely owed something more than another billion.

She remembers Zach saying to her: you're not happy unless you're sad; as if he could talk. But the sadness of it does suddenly well up, unbidden as always, and she gives a little laugh that threatens to swell into hysteria. It's been a good life, she thinks, life has been good to this flying ant, especially this, here, this is the best life I've ever had, and now she is laughing, as lights come on inside her, laughing hysterically, the best fucking life I ever had, shedding real tears as she turns away from the mirror. She can almost hear the footsteps, as if somebody were going from room to room inside her, through the mansion that is Aline Medlar, switching on branched chandeliers. She finds herself on the staircase in the hall, hugging the curve of the wall, wondering how long she's been there.

He's never let her down before. She climbs to the roof to see if she can catch sight of him, or let him catch sight of her. Steps out under the sky. It's a curious sensation: standing there in the dark, buzzing like a lantern at the top of the house. A lighthouse, she imagines her irises glowing greenly at the owls. Heat is now joined to light inside her, a curious burning that seems to begin at the pit of the stomach and radiate outwards in tingling spokes to her outer limits which are becoming increasingly hard to locate. A wedge appears to be driving in between the lobes of her brain as she becomes simultaneously an object to herself, visible as if from a height, a spotlit creature, and an intense and burning subject. Something I ate, the old self thinks, while the new elevated Aline is oblivious to vertigo, to animal dread.

Her feet approach the edge of the roof. Impossible to tell or even remember if the toenails are red. There's a small hurdle in the way. One foot tests its level top as she steps onto the parapet. She balances on the edge, breasting the dark. Now it's straightforward, a tightrope stretched across an abyss, a laser beam to infinity. She must simply place one foot before the other on the wire and that will bring her to the first halt, at the house just across the way where there's an important message to deliver. She can see a light on in there, a man she knows bent to a task.

The first stars guide her. She steps out into the night.

W alled garden

I have enclosed this space, planted trees, blinds, screens, trellises, so it is private, a rare luxury in this country. No eyes penetrate here, only sounds, the mindful slapping of flesh on one side where a young couple are assiduously making a baby, and the mindless smack of playing cards on the other, where a retired couple pass the hours in chaste bliss.

Brick red the wall, but also clay yellow, moss black, mud brown; warmed by sunlight, chilled by shadow, damp with ivy, glittering with parked dragonflies. The view is the same facing out or in:

BRICK MORTAR BRICK

MORTAR BRICK MORTAR

BRICK MORTAR BRICK

Inside: There may or may not be lilies white as the moon, as lies, as innocence; a mango, a fig, a pomegranate in flower, a serpentine folly and other gothic paraphernalia looming in the moonlight, a grapevine to camouflage a washline, a septic tank covered over with turf, a wilting pear, a tiny blood-red spider, a gate sweetly shut on the world.

Outside: Noise. The Goyal Cybercafe cum lending library. A lending library in Rosario, Argentina. Schoolgirls with hairy legs. A UP Roadways semideluxe bus. Its airhorn. A chow-mein takeaway. The Greenland Frozen Peas Factory. The People's Republic of China. A radium deposit twenty miles down that was active for six hundred thousand years 1.2 billion years ago. The liquor mafia. A pig girl. Ragpickers. Swine.

Impossible to believe in history walled in here; impossible to believe in this garden walled out there.

Slavery, Zach sneers, and also, evasion. Can it be both? Actually it's free work, you're not obliged to do it, *and* it's duty. Garden work roots you *and* frees you. Exhausted by evening, you step out onto the back veranda and there's a spill of sunlight on the bricks, a moistness in the air, a cool blue grey sky and fresh green leaves on the mulberry, and without warning you spring from the top step, just take off, ranting silent hosannas like a scabrous angel, as if the earth and everything in it were a gift meant only for you. You come thudding down on the lawn, of course, but the mood is still on you and again the divine madness returns to claim, all right, its slave.

Zach, who accuses me of living in a picture, imagines he can somehow escape the frame, and of course I would be happy if he did. But even my computer refuses to recognize an image unless it has a line around it. The frame is there, thank God; it's a refuge, a safe haven, because the battle is real and the lines are drawn. Class war. You come home and shoot the bolt lean up against the gate, spared. And the only intrusion is when the sun in winter warms the sheet iron and the gate pops in: *dhak!* Sometimes when I see a sadhu go by with his matted hair and his trident and his begging bowl I'm envious, naturally. Who wouldn't be? Who wouldn't shake off all attachments and simply walk away?

When I'm anxious for the future, I look up at the hornbill in the palm tree with a single areca nut in his beak, and think that's his whole pension too, his provident fund, his retirement package, his future, and then my fears are quelled. Not answered, put at rest. You have to sit quietly on your branch and offer up your self entire, to the world, to the universe, to the next passer-by.

In the meantime there's the spade. And the seasons. And the optical mouse. (Nerve damage, I've decided, not laser burn.)

Of course one travels, but I go to the mulberry tree for forgiveness when I come back. It has no words of reproach; it's enjoyed being there while I was gone. Enjoyed is a bit strong, but let it put out one new leaf – no promise of fruit – and let a ray of light shine through it, and you wonder. In that moment history, language, art, not to speak of time, look dull and do-nothing.

I lean against the wall. I feel the brittle stems of dead ivy against my arm, a gauzy rustle against my shirt as a creature struggles free. It isn't ivy. I've leaned against the dragonfly colony and mauled one. The broken creature flies up into the pomegranate tree beating against the new leaves. Will it live? Black, they choose the blackest bricks to rest on by day; they sleep by night, like us, if any creature with more eye than head may be said to sleep, in formation on the vertical plane, their wings dipped, all pointing the same way, up.

I look up at the sound of rain on the banana leaves and think of Wu Xinfu's 'Almost Nonexistent Garden'. This one's there all right but virtual, with millions of digits streaking invisibly down from St Petersburg and New York. Not one decent library in town, but every download is a miracle.

Clear History says a tab in the dialog box, and my finger hovers uncertainly.

W itch

'The locals say she was practising witchcraft.'

Inspector Bisht's right knee jiggles uncontrollably. He hasn't scented blood. It doesn't mean he wants the bathroom. It doesn't mean anything.

'People say all sorts of things.'

Mrs Wilding feels free to answer for her son since he is being questioned at home. She for one is glad that what happened happened. Not glad, relieved. Zaccheus is safe from the dowager's clutches. If he had any sense he'd have seen long ago that that young Trotter girl was a picture and brought her home, here. She's not going to be on the shelf long. This Mr Bisht seems a nice gentleman.

'Her face and arms were covered in boot polish.'

Zach goes to say something but is silenced by a look from his mother.

'We found a painting in her house which had been stolen. So there was some connection with criminals.'

Mrs Wilding, whilom music teacher, knows the value of silence. Several bars of it fill the drawing room.

'You supplied her meals?' Bisht says eventually.

'Some days. She liked our khana.'

303

'Theirs is different, no?'

'Ours is half and half, not too spicy, not too bland. You can stay and see,' she invites him, looking at her watch. 'In this house there's always an extra place.'

'No, no, I won't, thank you. The *Mrs* ...' Bisht's eyes go round and stern.

That's when Mrs Wilding knows it's safe. It's not her cooking he's afraid of. She looks at Zach. He looks shattered, poor boy, but he was sound asleep that night, she's sure. Besides, he might pull, but he'd never push.

'We think we have the culprit,' Bisht says, standing up. 'A seasoned man. Right now they are breaking his knees in Kotwali. He'll confess.'

They go out to the portico where Bisht's moped stands, small and silver, like a dawn horse.

'What do you feed your chrysanthemums?' Bisht would like to know. He's hanging over a lemony pincushion bigger than his face.

'You like the "Paris Daisy"? It's my favourite too. Mulberry compost, and pigeon droppings. But you must steep the droppings till they're the colour of weak tea or the tips will burn.'

'"Paris Daisy",' Bisht takes a note and turns to go. 'You make cuttings in winter?'

'In a month or two. After the first frost.'

'Oh yes,' Bisht remembers and unhooks the tiffin carrier from the moped handlebar. 'This is yours, I think. We examined the contents, just routine, and there was nothing ...' He wonders whether *amiss* would be polite and decides to leave it out.

He mounts the moped a second time.

'For the cuttings January is all right?'

'Perfect.' Mrs Wilding would give him whole gardens.

X *is for* kiss

See also X = target

X = kiss

In the morning I find Manda in the mesh room staring at the wall. She won't speak, just looks frightened, no, terrified. She's lost her voice. But she can point, to the open door, to her bare ankles. It takes me a minute to understand what happened; she has to get up and point to where the wire mesh was cut.

Now it sinks in I'm frightened for her, but also grateful she's spared, seemingly unhurt.

'What happened, Manda?'

Silence. I ask and ask and she just looks at me.

This is the chatterbox, the Vox, Lady Decibel herself. I think back to a day when she was three, a regular bawler. It's evening and I'm taking the night train to Delhi, my bag still unpacked, things strewn over the bed. I'm late. Across in her room she's sensed a departure although I haven't broken the news yet. 'Tell her just before you go,' Olivia says, to save us some pain, though she knows she'll catch it when I'm gone. No sooner has she uttered the words than a wail goes up from Manda, who has seen through the plot and wishes to punish us, me for going and Olivia for abetting.

The wail spreads in sobbing heaves from the epicentre, a

307

voluptuous shout of pain. She is being abandoned, she is heart-broken, she will never forget this suffering, never forgive this betrayal. I am in a state myself, brought on partly by my indecision: should I have told her earlier, warned her days ago? Also I have a chancy journey to the train station before the real journey begins. I have a hundred things to think of before I go. Now this din. I want to kill her. If it goes on one second longer I'll pick her up and tear her to ribbons. Shut up! I scream back at her. She doesn't stop. I rush to the bed where she's lying, looking at the ceiling and screaming mechanically without, it seems to me, especial sorrow. *Shut* up, I grab her. Shutupshutupshutupshutup shut*up*! I bend over her and cover her mouth with mine. Silence. The noise first muffled then extinguished like a candle. Success, but in an act of pure aggression I stick my tongue in that small mouth. There, you little animal. A gobstopper, the kiss of war.

This morning I'm trying to coax a sound out of the same mouth. What is it, Manda, you can tell me.

Silence.

It's the shock, I think; it'll pass. I want to touch her into speech but she turns her head away into deeper silence. I'll take any noise now, I want that *sa re ga* to fill the house. I stand up, turn aside in despair. If shaking would work I'd shake sound out of her. I sit down again. Only talking will do it. Now I must either force out words which stick in my throat or call a woman friend. My tongue wilts, defeated ten years on. By midday I know I must get help. Maya comes over, a former lover, and womans the story out of her. The kiss of peace.

I get the facts at second hand. The dreaded *worm*! One bung digit and the cat jumped the wrong way. Here's what happened.

X = target

Half-past three. Even the dogs are asleep. A palm frond rattles to the ground in the dark and lies there like a severed arm.

Manda turns over in her sleep and pillows her head on the soft muscle just above the elbow. It's not often she dreams about singing: tonight there is a white stave in the centre of a dark page with a complex series of demisemiquavers that she must negotiate at speed. She's on some kind of vocal steeplechase that puts you through every conceivable pace and this hurdle is one she's always skipped. Danger attends on its execution. It can be circumvented but shame attaches in some way to its avoidance. Don't forget me, it smirks. I exist.

Out on the street a figure detaches itself from the shadows, alerted by a bent stick left on the verge. The figure wheels like a drunk to the hedge and fetches up at the indicated gatepost. By the light of the streetlamp it finds the cross the pig girl X-ed there: on target.

Gilgitan springs up onto the wall gripping the security rail and vaults the creeper with its bell-like blossom concealing iron spikes, landing softly on the lawn. He slips along the brick walk towards the house, ignores the grey flight of steps that leads to the front veranda, and crosses to the side of the house where the water tanks and bathrooms are. Here, where sewage pipes meet inspection pits and brooms and drain cleaners and bottles of acid huddle in dank corners, is the sweeper side of the house, invisible even to the inhabitants. He always chooses that approach to a back yard, always a narrow gulley with a cement sullage drain you can tiptoe along instead of stepping on shingle. Behind the house is a bare patch with the remains of a kitchen garden. He crosses the crusted soil and stands on the far side facing the house with his back to the wall so no one can come up behind him.

Sometimes he can judge a house simply by the way it sits there, sometimes he has only to cast an eye around the garden. This one says, thrifty: there'll be no jewellery left around, no cash, maybe an ornament or two. Maybe he should just jump the wall and try next door. He needs cash and then he must lie low somewhere. They raided Paltaniya's, the pig girl said. You just keep moving, Gillu. He yawns briefly, nervous, not sleepy, though he is tired. Houses are strange. His was always a hovel, not even an outhouse. But a roof's a roof. For a while it was a tent, a piece of canvas across a pole, before his father bought a load of demolition asbestos sheets, but he has known flattened kerosene tins, bits of board, slate, chairbacks, chickenwire under straw, palm thatch, tarpaulin, and he has slept in countless builders' huts of dry brick and black polythene.

Houses like this are in another league; he will never in his natural life enter one by the front door, that he knows, not by day, in day clothes. He looks down at his langot, at the piece of gutstring knotted around his neck, the little penknife dangling from it, and imagines himself pressing a doorbell like that and almost laughs out loud. He's been in dozens of such houses, houses crammed with things, useless, shitty shiny things he scorns to touch. He has watched their owners asleep, judges, commissioners, superintendents of police, chairmen, engineers, chemists, watched their breath come and go, seen their underbellies, rolls of spongy flesh under moist singlets, their soft wives turning over with a clink of bangles, their fat children who sometimes wake and see him standing there and go round-eyed and rigid when he raises a warning finger because they know you do not disobey a troll.

He stirs himself. Is that a head above the parapet or coil of rope? There's a fancy bicycle leaned against a pole on the back veranda, a towel rack, an air conditioner; the sort of people who might leave a door open. Wait a minute. He looks again around the garden. Hasn't he been here before? Now he thinks he recognizes the grassed-over mound of the septic tank, the way it hills. Yes, he came here with and Chhanga and Phuljari, surely. No, it's a false memory. Now he knows what it is. He went once with his father to clean out a septic tank in a house with such a back yard. His father stuck his arm up the Y-pipe of an inspection hole, squelching through shit to find the blockage. It was his father's arm, that bare arm he has never forgotten, disappearing down that pipe with its bubbling yellow mash of filth.

The thought brings him to his feet. Why can't people unclog their own shit? He leaps straight up onto the boundary wall like a cat and sits there a moment, sniffing. No dogs. He jumps down onto shingle, toes first to muffle the sound. But this compound has an unexpected gate down the side between back and front yards; it's at the bottom of the external roof stair, a blank iron door set under a bricked lintel and bolted from the other side.

He must swing himself up by the banister and down the last few steps, slight inconvenience, into the walled garden. A small grassed oval with a winding gravel walk he steps across twice, and a queer pointless serpentine wall with a rounded arch. He peers through the archway: a crazy stone path that leads nowhere, flowerpots stacked in tilting towers, a goblin city. He stands a moment in the arch and studies the house: this one will have a computer, china, pictures. He should simply jump the back wall into a third yard and try the house behind. But he doesn't. He squats down right there and studies the windows, the skylights, the doors. The bricks behind him are unplastered, rough grained; in parts where the mortar oozed it digs into the flesh of his back. He clasps his legs with both arms and sits there in the dark, a hunched idol with eternity spread before him. Once he lifts his chin off his knees and looks up at the sky. Mars winks at him, red and silver with a flush of red gold. Three fifty-three, it reminds him, out of eternity. Get on with it or go home.

No, keep running, Gillu.

Still he sits considering, his eyes now lowered to the house. Can he have become addicted to this sort of interior, can he want simply to be among pictures and that sort of stuff? God help him! He catches himself thinking and likes that. He likes to sit and consider and watch himself thinking. He's had time to reflect. He has sat in countless backyards at three in the morning and reflected on the nature of houses and their contents, human and not. He smiles when he considers that the inhabitants if they were to come across him in the street, in broad daylight, would not give him a second thought, the kind of second glance you give a man who interests you by the way he carries himself or the way his thoughts have shaped his face. These folk simply don't see him. She saw him, the American, looked at him, for that alone he could have loved her. But this lot, if he were to block their way they'd just shout or jump or run but they would still not look, much less credit reflection in such a creature. The thought lends his speculations a certain piquancy and he catches that too and likes it.

He stands up, recrosses the little back lawn, and makes for the other side of the house, walking on his heels to hush the gravel. Now a narrow bricked passage along some kind of converted portico. His feet leave brick for stone; now a mosquito mesh wall. He slips the gutstring over his head and unclasps the knife. One cut, a few inches, so he can reach in and undo a latch. Such elaborate window grilles, such simple doors! People are strange. He inserts the point of the knife into a tiny mesh square just above the door handle. Softly he saws on a single strand of wire till it gives; then the next, then the next. He sets up a rhythm: it could be a cricket fiddling. One thumb keeps the pressure on the mesh, as each strand yields. Inch by inch the mesh parts. He pushes in and folds it back to allow three fingers in. Finds the bolt and works it gently up and down, sliding it as he goes. A little careless now because it's late. Very soon the muezzin will call and the robin will grow restless and early morning walkers will clear their throats in the dark. He should already be heading off. Madness to be caught like this. He'll just take some thing small, anything, from this room, and go.

The bolt slides back, he pushes open the door.

There's a bed right there, not three feet away, with a girl on it. She's awake. She's staring at him, terrified.

He lifts a finger to warn her, finds it's the penknife. Lets the point hold her gaze while he runs his over the contents of the room. Nothing. A nothing room. Then he sees an iron ladder in the corner that leads up to a gap in the ceiling. He nimbles up it, and finds an airy loft at treetop level. The oratory. Bare in the grey dawn light with a table at the centre and a lacquered box on it. He springs at the table and lifts the lid.

A tiny painted woman on one square inch of ivory.

He brings his face right up to hers in silent adoration. She'd fit snugly in his palm. What are you waiting for, Gillu?

Let her be.

He's down the ladder in seconds. The girl still frozen there. Come on, rich girl, I haven't got all day. Something, anything. He looks down at her, her bare neck, nothing there, her bare arms, no bangles, no rings on her fingers. The knifepoint steady, he reaches with his free hand for the sheet that covers her lower half and tugs it aside, then, still holding her with his eye, finds a bare foot and runs his fingers up the ankle. Yes. Grips the payal and pulls sharply; the silver chain breaks. Now the other foot. She offers it, waits for the tug.

Then he's gone.

Y *is for* Y ellow

See also Y ak, Y eti

Y ellow 1

I get the South Asia treatment at JFK, but my heart is singing. His heart is not in it either, this immigration officer on the verge of retirement, and how is he to know I will joyfully submit to any indignity, up to and including martyrdom, or at least rectal search, because Manda has found her voice.

It happened in midflight above Greenland. Around midnight I felt my arm gripped and tugged towards the window.

'Papadumb.'

I sat up, wide awake instantly and looked at her. Clearly she didn't know she'd spoken out loud. We'd got so used to communicating by other means over the past week, the whisper was an explosion in my ear.

'Look.'

I was still looking at her, but little by little I grew conscious of what it was she meant. The aircraft wing was on fire. No, the yellow glow was moonlight, silver and gold on the wing and on the ice far below. A zigzag of white coastline, and slipping from fjord to fjord the moon, a bright half-moon in black water. All the generations of men before us, all the fathers and daughters who ever lived, could only dream of such a sight. We watch in silence till the scene drifts away. Now silence is blessed; we preserve it.

Tumult inside me, multitudes exulting so even the turbulence we run into is nothing, because it's been a day of gifts. Late last night the surdy engineer called to say he's sorted out the hard disk, retrieved every file. *Red* is safe. I look around the plane for God but he's elsewhere; then the turbulence gets bad and I know he's just taking a little back. I'm Jonah, root cause of these hiccups, but there's no way I can explain this to the crew. Manda sleeps on, her beautiful head on my shoulder.

Olivia meets us in the concourse and they fall into one another's arms, Manda's every sob new minted. Then we embrace, the Aztec and I, almost formally, like treaty chiefs. Love glancing off Manda and falling on the icefields of six years. She's driving a Saab, so yOGabydancing.com can't be all washed up. Breakfast is lox and bagels, a nod to me, lunchtime we drive out again. She slows by a diner.

'You want your beef barley and pastrami on rye?'

She's telling me she remembers a story that predates her by a decade.

'And the *New York Times* on the date of issue?' Manda pitches in because she wants to hear it again.

So we stop and do that, to commemorate a day thirty years old. The newspaper kiosk man, then unborn, is from Punjab; he has family in Dariya Dun. He says he's going back when he's made his million. We both grin and know he's lying, an immigrant to his backbone, as American as Olivia, as my Manda. When he hears I have just a month he looks concerned and says he knows a good immigration lawyer. No, seriously, he pleads, all worked up now, and I can see he's not lying. His heart's here, he's not a brownnose, not a costume Indian. I want him to prosper. I buy a magazine as well.

We're in SoHo, among the galleries. I leaf through my *New Yorker*, look at the listings up front, another generation of pundits and sly puffers being oracular and wry by turns at the embarrassment of riches. Someone has to sort it out. At random we pick one, go in: an installation built with crashed hard disks, a whole skyline of floppies, dockyards of punched cards salvaged from some warehouse. I tell Olivia about the virus that almost killed *Red*; she shows interest, says nothing about remainder trays at Barnes and Noble.

It's harder for her to hide evidence of the new guy. No toothbrush or anything as careless as that, but a tone that brightens her voice and a way she has of turning her back when the phone rings at a certain hour. Afterwards she goes quiet.

'What's up?'

She doesn't answer.

'Did I say meat?'

'No, you said something worse.'

'There's a worse word?'

'Yes, and you've been using it ever since you got here.'

'What's that?'

'Nothing.'

I sigh. We've crossed this field before. 'I'm a writer, not a speaker.'

'Yeah, yeah, and you've used up all your words.'

'We both have.'

So I produce a picture instead. *The Painter's Family* comes to mind – now why should that be? I call it up on her notebook, call it down off the satellite, out of the belly of the mainframe where

Zee*bytes*.com has given me whole gigabytes of storage space, and I read from the early pages of this book. She says she's read my stuff before and why don't I write a normal novel for a change? Something that sells. It turns into a shouting match in the middle of which Manda, looking as adult as only she can, walks pointedly through the room searching for her headphones. So we cool off into a seminar on territoriality and end up sounding more than ever like treaty chiefs. 'The Azteca and the Anglo-Indian Share a Peace Pipe', by Charlie Russell. Then the phone rings again and she jumps up, bright as ever. I bridle and buck and begin to think about travelling west, to the wild expanses at the far end of the I-94 that I loved as a young man, but end up loitering in Central Park. When I remember Matisse. Too late for the great exhibition. I will never see the Picasso–Matisse show that attracted nine thousand visitors a day.

'Live here,' is her advice. 'You can go to MOMA any day of the week.'

I go there to look at one painting, but there's a crowd in front of it. The last time the crowd was in front of *Guernica* before it went home to Spain. It had a special chapel and wailing wall. Picasso's countryman and fellow Republican, Buñuel, was not among the worshippers. For its big words, its posturing and its naked propaganda, the filmmaker said, it ought (and given the subject he must have chosen his words) to be bombed. So I turn away from *The Red Studio* a little sadly but not inconsolable. What it is about originals that makes a fetish of them? I can call up the painting at any time and examine it more carefully than I could ever hope to on the wall. I can sit barechested in Dariya Dun, a little sweaty at the armpits but otherwise at my ease, and examine the nasturtium leaves in the black vase on the red table,

A and Z's table, at magnifications up to 1600% and know Matisse would have approved. (400% is best.)

The West notion palls, Manda has her music. It looks like there's a scholarship at the Julliard within reach. *Sa re ga* and *guruji* are vivid memories she's determined to stay loyal to, but loyalty is up against space, distance. Perhaps there's a guruji here. What's here for me? I shop for a coffee grinder, a claw hammer, a spirit level, a mechanical pencil-sharpener: those little engines the Americans make better than anyone in the world. And a couple of Californian reds. It's when I bring in the fresh Parmesan Olivia knows I'm serious about home. You could cut the silence with a cheese knife; each of us so chock full of our common past we can't trust our voices. She's better at holding her tears; I just nip out for some fresh air and find a wet shine on every light in Times Square.

On the last evening we eat at the Afghan place she spoke of. I choose it because I know I will never see the country just along the mountains with King Babur's grave on a knoll among the poplars. Olivia wanted to show me a Cajun watering hole but she knows we have okra in garden at home and gumbo comes out of a book. That night we kiss hard like the first time: I know she's/she knows I'm impossible to live with and impossible to live without.

On the way to the airport we stop at a plant nursery. At JFK I see the same official stamping passports and he lifts his eyebrows in a friendly way. So soon? I can see he's changed his mind about me. Now the look in his watery eye is forgiving, expansive: Give me your huddled masses. I nod, maybe next time, but he shakes his head. He can't see how anybody could not want to stay. He could be just tired. Most likely he's looking at someone behind me. I am too: Manda's face in the gap of the sliding glass doors.

My travelling companion is a Bengali doctor going to his ancestral village to sell a piece of land. How many patients to one doctor in his village, I ask him. He looks at me suspiciously.

'It's full of Bangladeshis.'

'Don't they need doctors?'

'Muslims are tougher. They have a meat diet.'

Banter. He's dealt with cavillers before, this man we trained up at some cost for seven years. Every year ten thousand like him take their training and gift it to the West. In a little while he will grow maudlin and patriotic and begin to lament the lack, no, the paucity, of research facilities at home. That's what drove him away, not the prospect of more loot. I go to the back of the plane to scrounge a seat. There's a whole row free: more legroom for the claret ash, whose spear-shaped leaves look freshly blooded; space between the toilets for exercise to appease the dark god DVT.

I come home to a pile of pigeon post and dust on the dining table which suddenly looks broader than the Atlantic. O's chair invested with St Elmo's fire, Manda's touch on every light switch.

Y ellow 2

On the hill above the battle (or the hunt or the god), beyond the standing corn and the field of flowering mustard in the middle ground, up above the two robbers and the snoring carter and the partridges and patient oxen flicking their tails, just where the white road bends at the hermit's cave, is the city, with children playing cockalorum at the gate.

It is always yellow. It is what glows like a pot of gold at the horizon, like the east before sunrise, like a pear in a porcelain dish. Its battlements and crenellations are ochre, its roofs terracotta, the pennants vermilion. Old sandal the windowsills, the bricks loam, the eaves fresh jaggery, variants all of yellow. Long after you've tired of the exploits in the foreground, this corner of the painting haunts you, these two square inches of yellow. Let black armour fill up the front, let red stream from the animals of the hunt: after the alarms and excursions are over the eye returns by corn and cockalorum to the city.

Why?

Because all other colours are action; yellow is repose. After the song of red, after the scrum of brown and blue and green, after the edging of black which bounds character and incident the way death shadows life, after all afters, there is the tranquillity of yellow. Only its close cousin white stands closer to undifferentiated light. Tiring of deeds and derring-do, of busy narrative, the eye longs to return to contemplation and simple doing.

I feel it myself now as, with great impatience, I prepare to step outside story and live again. The waiting city is a repository of simple repetitive living, all the little jobs on hold, some for months (the renewal of my driver's licence for one) waiting for the grand action to cease. After the romance of red, an obsession with a bit of lace, the blessed flatness of the quotidian. Yellow is the return of equipoise, when emotion is once again equal to action. It is the promise of peace (and also the hope of prosperity: that pot of gold). No wonder it was appropriated for angels and haloes and heavenly light. And cities on a hill, or, like ours, in a valley.

Y ak

We are walking to heaven, five blackshorts from the old old days. It is somewhere up there in the mountains where there is snow. Heaven is always cold. Our sacred wife goes ahead as always, showing us the way, then old Dhanush, then Buransh, maundering about beauty and revolution, then the twins, last of all me, Gillu. The dog died saving me. Death was stalking us in the Dreamforest and would have pounced, but Tharu turned and charged him. Faithful hound, he was taken! Many's the time he shared my bed and bone. He's gone to god.

Half the sky is black and thunderous, half clear where the sun is declining. The front of me, facing the mountains, is cool, the back hot. I think we are leaving heat behind, and mangoes. Again I must run to catch up. My sandals are a sight and when last did any of us stop to comb hair? Sometimes I think we are walking in a great circle and when we turn the next corner She will be waiting, my true wife, visible only to me, her brightness a lantern.

What if I ducked out? Would they miss me? The twins, who walk side by side, except on the most beetling ledge, when they have to be blindfolded and led, never look back. I can't remember when our sacred wife last looked at me. Or when I felt those dugs. I could pretend to mend a sandal, then just melt into the forest. Do I really want to go to heaven? I feel I've been there and this is better. These gentians, that dove. Let me think a little.

I have left them. The queue, the we-six from which I once hung like a tail. The little finger on the cohorts' hand, spare. Now I taste for the first time the pleasures of solitude, and the fears. Alone, weirdalone, looking behind me, ahead, on either side, at every step. I know I should have stayed with the sum (six always including me, even as their seniority, marginal in the case of the twins, shut me out). I should have kept up, tagged along even at the cost of a little rank. But what it is to be the sidekick on the edge of heaven, only I know. Or only Tharu trotting at my heels truly knew, one respectful eye forever cocked, half obedient to the instincts that had him eat grass when sick or go round and round chasing his tail before bedding down in long grass, half drawn to me and mine, his celestials. And he threw it away. All things considered, then: I did well. *To turn aside* – that actual moment of stepping away – such relief you could scream. And scream I did, into a cave, a day after I was sure they were out of earshot. Nothing ever felt so good.

So this is better. Better than nothing, but of course soon enough I'll want more than this and then where will I be? Then I must find an earth mother, a snake wife to sleep with and go into some nights, vault over with the whole length of my pole and come deep inside of, to sow some fresh death in so we can build a new paradise. Let her be the pig girl or let her be the American. This time I'll make sure heaven is not in the snows. I'll take her so hard the grass will burn up. Home is here, where it's hot. Let there be heat and shade, game, a bitch, a spring, a fig tree, a thicket for poles, a melon patch, and high stone walls. A low round entrance, a large rock, red.

Then come in search of me, goddess, with your eyes that say *Kill me, or be killed.*

I'm here.

Come on foot, or slithering, or if it pleases you, on a yak.

Y eti

Olivia.Gutierrez@yOGabydancing.com

> *O*
>
> *What would I do there?*
>
>> To sit in New York making Indian noises
>> Become their yeti, be their dancing bear
>> Run them up a handy hairshirt – when
>> They already *have* their wounded Indians there!
>
>> *No. I think Manda'll see the sense of it too. I'm writing a*
>> *proper letter, recycled paper to satisfy her green sensibilities.*
>> *My own are worn to shreds so I sit in the shade of the*
>> *balsam poplar and let its balm go to work. The heart's just*
>> *fine, never fear, but the claret ash died. I brought Zach home*
>> *a sycamore for when he's feeling low and a couple of reds*
>> *for when he needs to get a bit higher. On second thoughts I'll*
>> *keep the reds. Big kiss for each of you.*
>> *N*

Back comes a stinger from the net, the low net, tennis among
her many accomplishments.

N

Big kiss for you too sugarbun but you really think you can just walk away like that? One of these days you're going to have to bend a little and check the lock on that gate. What do they call it, a kutcha lock? Nice word. Fake lock. It lets you pretend, to yourself because mostly no one else cares, except for your Manda, and me, a little bit, still, that you're on the verge of some kind of salvation or sainthood or maybe even direct translation, Mr Author, when really all that happens on the inside is a kind of waiting, maybe a kind of wasting, of at least one life.

One more thing. Those ecstasies. Are they a way of doing nothing about your heart? Are you in denial?

Go ask your mulberry.

O

Z *is for* Z accheus

See also Z eebytes.com, Z ipphone,
Z-zzzz, Z om

Z accheus

Barista, Wednesday.

I'm late, Z's waiting, chin cupped in his hands. Slate-grey moleskins, blank T-shirt. I'm wearing an apricot shawl with a border of crossbones and carrying a small cane.

He's not quite over the whole red business, I can see: still looks drawn and melancholy. It's our first meeting since I got back. To cheer him up I tell him my coming-of-age story. My twenty-first birthday and I get out of the Greyhound looking for the real New York. Yes, they have no pastrami, they tell me at this diner, but they have special sandwiches: curried egg à la Inde. The kiosk outside is fresh out of the *Times*, but the guy says I can have yesterday's for free. God's truth. Z smiles his glum smile (the look that first drew A) and sucks at the straw in his empty glass. I reorder.

He tells me A was taken home. (Did she travel on the same plane that carried Manda and me? While we looked down on Greenland she was in the hold?)

Then he tells me of a haunting.

'Last night. I was on the roof as usual, walking up and down when I heard this sound from the back veranda, like a door being forced. The back door sticks, OK? I have to leave it open when I go up onto the roof – the staircase is outside.'

'I know, I know.'

'The noise was of someone opening the door who didn't know about the sticking. So it couldn't possibly have been my mother and in any case she sleeps like a log and this was about three in the morning. So I went back down straight away and bolted myself in and then went from room to room to make sure there wasn't an intruder. Not a soul. Then I hear this page being turned in the dark. I get a hell of a scare. But it's just the table fan blowing on a book my mum left open. So I go to bed as usual and just as I pull the sheet up under my chin I hear this strange tick-tock, tick-tock. And again, coming closer, tick-tock, tick-tock, tick-tock. I lift my head and see this figure in the shadows. All in black, a sort of old-fashioned gown from a hundred years ago, shapeless, or maybe just a triangle, an isoceles triangle.'

He steeples his index fingers.

'Coming towards me. A walking triangle, rocking from side to side. Tick-tock, tick-tock. And then I see the red hair and I know who it is. The girl in the painting. Arms hanging straight down, and a hatchet in one hand. She's at the foot of the bed and still coming, looking straight at me. I'm lying there frozen, my skin like Braille. She comes right up to the side of the bed and stops her rocking. Stands there staring at me, then slowly bends over and peels off the sheet. Unbuttons my nightshirt. Cuts out my heart and eats it raw. Then she takes hold of my hair and lifts the hatchet.'

He holds me with his eye. 'But it's not a hatchet, it's a book, a yellow book. And she bends over me and whispers something in my ear and smiles for the first time. And gets up and walks slowly away. Rocking, tick-tock, tick-tock.'

RED

Zach sits there playing with his straw, the coffee glass sweating.

'Words of wisdom, old son?' I fish. I don't press because it's the longest story I ever heard him tell; notes, not words issue from him.

He shows his teeth for the first time since Aline, and taps the left ear.

'She spoke to the wrong side.'

Back to one line. Then since we're trading ghost stories I tell him of the scare I got one morning just before dawn. I had been working all night at the computer writing up the soot ceremony of the blackshorts. Went to wash my face and as I turned on the tap at the basin I noticed something on my left wrist: a soot-black smudge. That shook me. When I examined the skin closely I found it was a sweat mark off my steel watchstrap.

I think telling his story has helped. He still looks wounded, but then he was hurt into the *Nocturnes*. He says the music is better than anything he's done so far, less theoretical, but is pained by the gap between what he imagined and what he managed. Aren't we all. That's OK too. He's young and ready to spit in God's eye. Bit of spark, bit of spunk. Still torn between solitude and sex, black and red. Like God in the beginning, sick of being alone, begins to think and suddenly finds himself Object as well as Subject. S/O, as my tax form says, son of. Or Significant Other unto himself.

He still manages to imply that all this is an operetta he is writing, the light opera of my life, but that's youthful hubris too. What he needs is to go wandering, to live among strangers again for a bit. He's afraid he'll only find himself lying in wait there, but at least the frame will be new.

'You could start a music magazine,' I suggest. 'Isn't it time we had our own? Bugger *Metronome*. And Risingholme while you're about it. Go independent.'

'Is this Nationalism?'

'Small n, Zachariah, small n. The big I is for Internationalist. In-between. We're hyphens, you and I.'

'And the big N?'

'*Your* narrator, don't forget.'

Just putting him in his place. Sometimes I think this arthritic valley depresses him. Not that he'll go far. He'll probably find a woman on the Net, be lured into a chatroom, and repeat all his mistakes to date. But he'll return to his corner when the bell goes. Whoever she is I suspect she'll have to come here; he couldn't live without the call of the coppersmith. But she'll cut the apron strings for him, be his fate healer. More likely he'll die a bachelor, my faithful Ariel. Grace notes descending on his grave.

It's him or me. My money's on him. He'll stay the course: a scamfest dipster he might be but he's not a cocksucker.

It's me I worry about. How do I grow a new tail? Do I change the lock, go far away, or go a long way into something, turn inside out, moult this skin? O doesn't realize how much her natural man's changed. Did she create a monster on the rebound with her fantasies of the definitive organic male? A golem who can bond with software but not his wife? Married to his machine, always looking to download an angel. Now she knows two things for sure: I'm still interested and I'm not about to go and live there.

When I got back I found the garden changed. A bit of outside come in, a bit of inside got out. I shut the gate and drew the latch and stood there exulting: free, *free*! But the mulberry was not convinced. I cocked an ear. The neighbours, the purest fiction to me while I wrote, were back. Slap went the young flesh, smack went the old cards.

So now what? Raze the walls, go naga? But the snakes have fled, and black is not bottomless. Red was, for a year, now even orange looks doubtful. Black-red I find I misconstrued. I've just learnt from a Barista newspaper that the annual flight of ants is a nuptial flight: they're not despairing, they're pairing!

Topheavy N, sidewhelmed. Am I toppling over, turning Z?

Right now he looks sadder than ever. I invite him home to share the Californian reds and right then I remember what I forgot to buy. Racking my brain in Macy's for something absolutely crucial, now it strikes me: a *corkscrew*! The old one's dead, pulled straight, and Dariya Dun won't rise to one. So no reds: we'll drink English Wine as our shops say, spirituous liquor under a screwtop cap. Eat steamroller: that's a surdy with a tandoor tied to a roadworks machine.

I let him pay for the coffee, fair's fair. Tomorrow I'll celebrate the end and wine him, maybe borrow a corkscrew. All in all it's a good feeling, this almost thereness. An end to magic. Freedom, for now. Not a breeze, just a gentle welling up of air all round. Little notes to myself crop up in odd pockets. *Cite Jack Flam, Matisse scholar nonpareil*, and *Paul Polansky gipsy webmaster*. Other notes are just remnants, scribbles that put you sharply in mind of this or that character. I think of Aline on that parapet, high as a kite on the pig girl's truffle, stepping out into the darkness. But then A is always stepping out into the unknown, one foot stuck out over the abyss, while Z is always hunched over his unfinished task. I think of O too. Too often. My Omega. Coming home hasn't cured me but she has her life and I have mine and life has priority over love. And M. Mandra, Matisse, Marguerite. All the M's. Who else?

Z eebytes.com

I dial up BSNL and go to check my mail. Run an eye over the headlines.

Holemeal heiress slashes out. Red Medlar St Pierre, granddaughter of painter Aaron Medlar, and surprise heiress to the Holemeal healthy donut fortune, was today held in St Petersburg, Russia, for damaging a Matisse painting in the Hermitage museum worth millions of dollars. Medlar St Pierre, nineteen, was remanded in custody for allegedly slashing Matisse's famous canvas, *The Painter's Family*, with a Stanley knife found by museum guards on her person. She did not deny the act, merely repeating that she did it because the painting, a classic moment in twentieth-century art, was there.

Was Jesus a Kashmiri?
New notes from Hitler's bunker
Serial killer's plea: lock me up, throw away the key

One message in my inbox. I doubleclick so fast the mouse ignites.

N

yOGabydancing sold.

How does www.OliveGroveHeartcure.com grab you?

Be my agent?

O

So we go onto Messenger:

>And the guy on the phone?

>That was the buyer, silly.

Z ipphone

She grasps the sleeping pig's ear and speaks into it as into a cellphone, using both voices. Cellophane breadwrapper cap on her head, red.

You weren't supposed to come in, Gillu.

I pulled out.

Not soon enough. You left a little boy in there.

Don't worry.

You used something?

No.

Did you use something with her?

No.

What was special about her?

Just.

You gave her the painting for safekeeping, right?

Right.

She would have flown away anyway.

Yes.

So I blew her away for you, the bitch. Pinch of black snuff in her tiffin carrier. No truffle like the black one under the mulberry.

It had six piggies running in circles one time. Gillu? Next time come in the back way. What did you see in her anyway?

Girl, you talk too much.

OK, bye. Gillu?

Let him go walking, she knows he'll be back. Just to hear what she whispers in his ear. *Split me open, Gillu.* Only he can do that. She presses the Clear button, a fat tick, the way she's seen people do. The sow gets up and lumbers away.

Uncle! she salutes me. The cellophane cap wards off the evil eye, and men.

We see her and we don't. If she were cleaner we'd chase her.

There's an autorickshaw drivers' strike so I end up walking home from Barista past the jail. The nation's leaders sat behind those walls writing their fusty epics and came out to garlands, shake on it, *tovarish*; the other wretches had to pick up the pieces. What's it take, guts or grace? We're the inheritors. We cannot begin to imagine the wretchedness that sustains our lives.

Somewhere behind that wall is G, kneecapped by the cops. He'll never walk straight again. He filled my tyres once at Race-course chowk. Tiled my bathroom. Got a lungful of fine clay dust for his pains. He's in for a long stretch. The naga painting Aline had in her possession was traced to him. Inspector Bisht's detective work, using stylistic analysis of niche paintings in the valley, especially one at Paltaniya's house. And the Kangra miniature was returned to its home. There's a do-gooding NGO that encourages painting in jails, but I suspect G won't oblige.

The painter's sense of wonder is renewed every night – that's what black is for. Queen of colours, Matisse called black.

Z -zzzz

In his cell Gilgitan dreams of leaving this city which just kicks you in the ass. He chews a bitter cud. Vinod turned informer, who would have thought? The family's broken up; well, he himself preferred to go out alone when he could. He tried to quit too, but where do you hide from a goddess? The last time he was in jail he waited for Nagouri's revenge but she let him get away. (Phuljari died instead.) She was just saving him for a more delicious fate.

But there are places where even a goddess can't follow you. He'll never vault again, but he can close his eyes.

There: black, alone.

Hup.

Flying!

RED

He's over the wall. He lands on all fours and is up and running. Through a familiar landscape, the kind he knows from trucks. Trees, thin black pencils, flash past, bushes like the club on a playing card. Now he slows down, panting, falls in with a river that winds like a blueblack snake. Pauses at a long boat among the reeds but it's upstream he wants to go. Sits on a rock, cups his hands to drink, dips his heels in, then starts up again. By nightfall he's reached the hills, gently swelling hills, green as a green pigeon's breast, or the pig girl's. Taking her, o god, taking her. *Rip me open, Gillu.* I'm yours. Scorching the grass, torching every bush. Breasting the stars.

His feet leave prints in the white moondust but he casts no shadow. A man walking for his life, all his life, singing.

Z om *variant of* **Dom**

A man; a human being.